Wife Consultant

Colin Diyen

Langaa Research & Publishing CIG
Mankon, Bamenda

Publisher:

Langaa RPCIG
Langaa Research & Publishing Common Initiative Group
P.O. Box 902 Mankon
Bamenda
North West Region
Cameroon
Langaagrp@gmail.com
www.langaa-rpcig.net

Distributed in and outside N. America by African Books Collective
orders@africanbookscollective.com
www.africanbookcollective.com

ISBN:9956-728-63-2

Dedication

To Jude and Valentine Diyen

I also want a few special persons who have been working on my books to know that I really appreciate their contribution and will always be grateful to them. I want to thank Mrs. Ngalim Juliana Nakeh, Mrs Ezegha Florence Nchia, Miss Ngam Elizabeth Nange and Mr. Ndaba Godlove Yijofmein.

Isidore Irvine Diyen and Bah Maya Azah are always with me in spirit.

And

P. G. Wodehouse

1

Getting To Know Us

"Every woman needs a man." This statement is sounded in a melodious hit by one of our sisters. I wonder what you think about it however. While many women agree with this statement, others consider it as misguided. They declare that it gives macho men the reason to claim that they are indispensable and important. This school of thought strives to treat men with some degree of indifference and caution to prevent the men from taking advantage of them. But then, there are those sisters who virtually swoon and feel helpless in front of attractive men. Some of them even allow themselves to be pulled around by the nose and generally melt like butter when in the presence of a seductive man. In some cultures, women enjoy being bashed up by their men, a habit they consider as a display of love. In other parts of the world, women accept to hide their beauty behind ugly veils simply because husbands, who have very little faith in them, wish it. To me, old flabby and shapeless women could spend the rest of their lives behind veils and disguise their amoeboid structures, but young beautiful women should be allowed to display their attractive faces and beautiful smiles.

A friend of mine once said, virtually everything a woman does centres on getting men attracted to her. That is why she wants to look shapely, feminine, sexy and attractive. A woman may wear nice fragrances, the appropriate make up and manicure, and a cute dress simply because she wants to look good in the company of other women or make them jealous, but then the ultimate aim behind it all is to give the right impression to men. You may have a reservation to this statement given the fact that lesbians do dress and wear makeup too, but we are talking about women who accept that men have a part in their lives.

Yes, it is extremely difficult to understand a woman completely. A woman gives you the impression that she is fed up and disgusted with a man that has wronged her, and would want nothing to do with him. The next moment, with the slightest bit of pleading from him, you find her in the arms of the same man. Another woman is savagely beaten by a man who makes no effort to apologize and shows no remorse, yet she is still ready to hop into his bed.

I have never stopped wondering why many of my sisters prefer to stay back and let the man provide all the means of livelihood whereas they are fully capable of working and earning a good income on their own. Some women live as prostitutes and thrive on money offered by men, out of need. But then, many become prostitutes simply because they enjoy that way of life.

Another thing that I find difficult in understanding about some women is that they opt to play a submissive role, whether they have power, money or influence, and would always look for a man to lead or control them. They believe that a woman should play a subordinate and passive role, after all, women are known as the gentle sex.

On the other side of all these, there are women who think, act or behave as if men don't exist. Such women prefer to live their independent lives and fend for themselves. There are even women who go into a relationship with a man once in a while but always want to lead and dominate. Some women do not believe in being feminine and prefer to act masculine.

As for me, I like being a woman and prefer everything feminine. But being in the liberal field, and having the appearance of an experienced, and understanding female and mother, I find myself playing the role of consultant quite often to persons of my sex. The men should not be scared though, for I have no intention of pitting their women against them. But if you are handling your wife the wrong way, adjust and straighten up before she comes consulting me. That is where I am best as lawyer for cheated, deprived, neglected and distressed wives.

Hey women! Relax, read this book and learn. You will certainly, pick up a few hints from these stories and cope with your husbands.

Husbands! Also read and learn from these stories, ways of keeping your marriage happy ever after.

2

SIH

I was relaxing on the veranda, reading a good book by PG Wodehouse, and enjoying the way many women in his stories were taking advantage of men and obliging them to do certain absurd things to please the female sex. PG Wodehouse had a special affinity for women with red hair and I am sure he must have been a man of the world in his hay days.

My daughter Titi was relaxing with her friend Sih at one end of the veranda, poring over some feminine magazines and admiring dashing divas that were displayed on most of the pages. Some of them looked so thin and hungry that I wondered whether it was worth while being a model. However, the actresses and pop stars that also figured in the same magazine were not that scrawny and looked sizable.

Suddenly Titi gasped and called across.

"Mum," she said "listen to this."

"To what?" I asked putting down my book

When Titi wants my attention she does not want me to do anything else.

"There is something here in this magazine." she said "listen mum and let me read it out to you."

She turned to a new page and back again to the previous one.

"Are you reading?" I asked.

"Sorry mum," she said "here it comes; tips on how to keep your man satisfied; tips on how to keep your man to yourself; tips on how to satisfy your man fully in bed; tips on

5

how to make your man to like your house; the importance of finding out about your man's likes and dislikes."

"All that is in that magazine? I asked.

"Yes mum," Titi answered "and this is all hogwash. This magazine should talk more about women, female beauty, make up, cuisine and stuff like that."

"But it does dear." I said.

I had gone through the magazine before handing it to her.

"Perhaps," she said "but why the insistence on men? What is in a man? Why must women worry so much about men's preferences, dislikes and tastes?"

"You are still growing up to be a woman." I told her "When you become a full woman, you will discover that the centre of a woman's life is the man. A woman is not complete without the man. That is nature and we cannot do anything but comply with that."

"That is ridiculous mum." Titi replied "Men could be boring and many of them rather bring a lot of misery into women's lives. Look at this book I was reading where this bloke got two sisters and their mother competing for his attention. You also remember the film we were watching the other day where this Don Juan lured that young innocent girl into giving up her fiancé, just to end up abandoning her for a rich woman. I might still be inexperienced and understand very little about the ways of the world but we read about and watch the perfidy of men every day in books and films."

"Some women rather consider men as the source of happiness in their lives." I said.

"Do they really bring happiness into the life of a woman?" Titi asked doubtfully.

"When it is the right man of course." I said. "A woman will know no peace and happiness if she is saddled with the wrong man."

Titi looked a bit confused.

"You are still too young to understand it all." I said "And more to that, you have not really fallen in love yet with anybody."

I made this last statement looking keenly at Titi, hoping that I was right. It was no longer easy to tell when a young girl had had her first love.

"Do men also consider women as an important part of their lives?" Titi asked.

"They certainly do," I replied "only that they look at it from a different angle."

"I am sure men do not bother about women that much," Titi said "at least, not the way women fuss over them."

"Don't be that sure." I said "In Europe, men open car doors for women, offer them flowers and defend them when necessary, and even go on their knees to declare their love. In some African tribes, men pay dearly for a woman. I remember a Kenyan friend whose father was offered as many as a hundred cows for her."

I smiled at this last bit because I knew that the bride price was just like buying the woman, and she became some kind of property after that.

"I wonder whether I would allow myself to be sold like that." Titi said. "Did Dad pay lots of money to your parents to get a beautiful woman like you?"

"Things are changing now," I said "and some girls even elope with their men to avoid the bride price. Your father decided to respect tradition and his family met my family and discussed,"

"Mum, you are disguising things." Titi said "Anyway, talking about the attitude of men towards women, what of beating, cheating, and breaking women's hearts?" Titi asked.

"Some women make themselves cheap while others are simply unlucky." I said "In some cases, it is the woman that breaks the man's heart. I know many women who have tossed men around and still ended up happily married."

"Whatever the case, many more men break women's hearts." Titi said. "It makes it rather difficult to know when a boy is serious. You find girls crying at school often because a boy has abandoned them for a close friend of theirs. You can ask Sih what happened to her the other time."

Sih was Titi's bosom friend. She was quite a lovely girl and I liked her very much.

"There." I said "You have to acknowledge that often, it is the girl friends who present themselves as easy targets to their friends' boyfriends, while others actually chat the boys up."

"Why would a girl want to lure off a friend's guy?" Titi asked.

"Why would she even think of accepting if she is approached by her friend's boyfriend?" I asked "Men should be blamed for certain frivolous tendencies but women should be blamed even more for giving them a chance to take advantage of them."?

This topic did not come up again for a while and each time Sih came visiting, she would simply sit with Titi for hours watching celebrities over E channel on TV, or some replays of soap operas that had passed in the night. These were accompanied by girlish giggles and exclamations. Personally, I only watched Ghanaian and Nigerian films over TV and when I wanted to watch musical shows, I went for gospel music. I always wondered what these girls enjoyed in watching American celebrities discussing their wealth, their likes and dislikes, their love lives and their fabulous wealth. The celebrities even went as far as showing their dogs, their expensive cars, gold and diamond encrusted wrist watches and mansions. Ridiculous! The cost of one car could provide water for several villages in Africa. A simple wrist watch could be converted into money that could provide several health facilities, and one mansion could be transformed into several secondary schools in a third world country. The lucky fellows could not be blamed however because they simply believed that the world should be like that. One of them even declared that death was the main natural check to overpopulation, so the poor should be allowed to remain in poverty, hunger and sickness. That way, they would die faster and keep the world's population at an acceptable level.

I did not like Titi and Sih's choice of musical slots either. They preferred watching buxom black women wriggling and contorting their ample buttocks to the tune of Makossa, Coupé decalé or Congolese music. From these they would switch to half naked American artists shrieking off sexy tunes on stage. Give me gospel music any time. I could also appreciate some cool sounds.

Whenever they saw me engaged in household chores, Sih and Titi always jumped up to offer assistance. Things were quite fine that way and I was happy that God had blessed me with a good daughter, and provided her with a good friend.

It is this kind of closeness that a woman develops with her daughter that is good and helpful, not the relationship between father and daughter where he only steps in to spoil her or to sanction her savagely when he thinks she has gone astray. There are certain qualities and aptitudes in some women that men need to rely on when dealing with their

9

children, especially daughters. The sixth sense you might call it, but it is a fact that women are more gifted in reading their daughters than men. Pompous men who would not admit the female superiority in these matters, say women always exaggerate and raise hell over nothing. As usual, we allow such men to think that they are right, but we know better.

It is this aptitude to suspect or realize that something is amiss despite the absence of obvious signs, that enabled me to notice a change in Titi's and Sih's attitude whenever Sih came visiting. They assisted me in household chores as usual, passed their time together in front of the TV as usual, turned to their usual channels as usual and there was still some giggling. However, I noticed that their conversations with each other had become intense each time and they hardly even followed what was going on over the TV. What could be the problem? As a mother, I was bound to be worried.

If I told my husband, Akoni about this, he would simply laugh it off as one of those frivolous worries that women often entertain. After all Sih still came visiting, spent much time with Titi as usual and there was no quarrelling. I decided to pay more attention to the young women and make out what could possibly be cooking.

Titi was twenty and in University. Her friend Sih was twenty one and her classmate in university. Handling girls of this age is quite a delicate issue and the manner of approach matters much.

I contemplated sitting the two girls down and tactfully getting them to open up. But then, they may rather close up further. I spent two days thinking of a manner of approach. Fortunately for me Akoni was like most husbands. They hardly notice or worry about problems worrying their wives.

While I lay restless in bed worrying about my daughter and her friend, Akoni snored loudly, oblivious to my troubles.

After the two restless days I called my mother and told her everything.

"Why don't you simply call your daughter aside and ask her what is amiss?" She asked.

It was that simple and I had not thought of it yet. Of course, if I cornered Titi in the absence of her friend and broached the topic, she would certainly tell me everything that would enable me to intervene. What oversight on my part.

That afternoon I decided to act.

"Is your friend coming over today?" I asked Titi nonchalantly as she was removing a cup from which I had just had tea.

"No mum." She answered. "She does not have to come here every day, does she?"

"Well, no." I replied a bit embarrassed. "You two are so close and you spend so much time together, such that every observer would conclude that you see each other every day."

"True mum, if it were possible, we would love to see each other every day." Titi said

"And possibly stay together every day and maybe all through your lives." I said.

"Sure mum." Titi answered

"Have you ever considered the fact that a man could come in one day and split that tight bond between the two of you?" I asked.

This statement was intentional and I watched closely to see her reaction.

"No, don't say that mum." Titi said "I simply do not want to think of it."

11

"Well, do." I replied. "It is inevitable. On the other hand, your future carriers may take you far apart."

"Don't bring up such dark premonitions mum." Titi said. "For now we enjoy the company of each other thoroughly."

"Any way," I said. "I have something else to ask you. I hope you will be sincere with me."

Titi looked at me in surprise.

"I have noticed," I continued "that you two have some serious secret of yours which you are not sharing with me."

"What do you mean mum?" she asked.

"You two for the past two weeks or so have been having more serious exchanges each time she comes and even your girlish laughter during conversations is no longer that of delight from some exciting display on TV. The laughter now smacks of sarcasm, and what do you have?"

"You are imagining things mum." Titi said.

"Tell me honestly." I said sternly. "What have you girls been concentrating on these past weeks? What has been the topic of discussion?"

"It's girl talk mama." Titi said "You must understand. Let us talk about something else."

She was in a hurry to close the topic.

"I insist on you telling me what you and Sih have been up to." I said firmly.

"I say it is simply girl talk mama," said Titi "you won't understand us."

"I am a female too." I reminded Titi.

"But you are a full grown woman, a mum for that matter." said Titi.

"Sure," I said "but I was once a girl. Being older now does not change much. It does not make me less sensitive to problems and aspirations of young women like you."

12

"But you are a mum and mums often exaggerate, in the belief that they are giving their girls the best." said Titi.

"We passed through all these as girls and young women" I reminded Titi. "We equally made mistakes as young girls but we always realized our mistakes and corrected them. It is just that we want to help you circumvent those errors and avoid the misery we went through each time before adjusting. We are doing everything for your own good."

"There you go talking like a mum again." Titi said laughing.

I decided to change my approach.

"I can sense there is something wrong," I said in a cajoling manner "but something that I could easily handle if I knew what. Now Titi, open up. It is me your darling mother and not just some stranger from outer space. What is going on?"

Titi sighed, looked at me with pleading eyes and then spoke.

"A young man has proposed marriage to Sih and has been pushing virtually on daily basis for her to accept."

"Is there a problem with that?" I asked.

"She does not really like him." Titi said.

"Is that so?" I asked.

"And to make things worse, her mother is pushing her to accept. I am sure you would do the same and that is why I was hesitating to tell you." Titi said.

"Why does she not like him?" I asked "Is he not handsome?"

"He is." said Titi. "Besides, he is from a rich popular family and well educated."

"What is your friend's problem then?" I asked "Husbands are not easy to come by these days you know."

"There you go talking like a mother again." Titi said "Sih simply does not love him and love is important in marriage."

"Love could be developed." I said "Many wives today did not marry their dream guys but have adjusted and love their husbands dearly."

"I understand parents kind of imposed husbands on their daughters in your days and so you had no option but to develop love for the man". Titi said "These days we believe in love before marriage not after."

Men may have the tendency of telling their wives only what they remember to tell them but once a woman has information that is not detrimental to their marriage, her biggest urge is to tell her husband. Therefore, that night I told my husband everything, expecting much sympathy from him. I was disappointed.

"We live in a dynamic world," he said "with constant physical, moral, spiritual, and ethical changes that make it foolish to compare what obtained in your time to what should obtain during your daughter's time. Your mother was given to marriage as a very young girl and to a man she did not have the opportunity of choosing. When I married you, I was your choice kind of, but you finally succeeded in getting married to me because your parents did not object and rather encouraged you. If they had objected, I am sure you would have listened to them and our marriage would never have taken place. Today, if our daughter presents her choice to us we may not even have the right to object no matter what our opinion about the fiancé or groom would be."

"But what of the little errors in falling for a man, who ends up rejecting you, ill-treats you or disrupts your chances of getting hooked to the right man, or even abandons you with a pregnancy?" I asked "I don't think you could want that to happen to our daughter."

I thought he was trapped there.

"Many desperate women, devastated by unscrupulous men have been known to rise from the ashes like phoenixes to become great successful women." Akoni said.

"Are you saying that we should allow our daughters to grow up without guidance?" I asked angrily.

"Certainly not," said Akoni "but pushing her too far may cause her to react in an embarrassing manner."

What my husband said that night gave me food for thought, but then, a father faces his daughter from a distance either to discipline her or to spoil her. It is us mothers who must create a balance and bring a daughter up as a respectable, hardworking, tidy and complete wife. No mother wants to bring up a daughter that cannot cook good food for her husband, keep her house tidy or bring up her children the right way. A woman might be cheap or sexually promiscuous, close to the level of a kleptomaniac and keep a sordid and untidy home, but she would always want her daughters to be intelligent, faithful to her marriage, tidy and trustworthy.

The next day I could not help intruding into Titi's conversation with Sih.

"Would you like a drink, Sih?" I said as I poured myself a drink of orange juice and moved to occupy the seat next to hers in the living room.

Sih was surprised. Each time she came visiting, her friend Titi took full care of her. Once in a while, I had rather asked her to help serve me something whenever I wanted to relax, so my question sounded something out of the ordinary.

"Thank you auntie." she said, still looking embarrassed. "But Titi is already taking care of that."

I could not help looking at Titi's face too. It looked like I had interrupted them in some rather very exciting conversation.

"I hope you don't mind me sitting here with you," I said "even adults often need such youthful company to exchange ideas."

"No problem auntie." Sih said.

She was very polite. Titi for her part looked cross. My daughter loves me very much but at this particular instance she was certainly considering me as an unbearable intruder. That is why our daughters often love their fathers better, given the fact that they are not always present when they need time with their friends.

I ignored Titi's countenance.

"Sih, please excuse me for bulging into what you may think does not concern me," I said carefully "but you see, I am virtually like your mother. I am old enough and experienced enough to know what is good for you and advise you correctly. If you have any problems, please feel free to approach me. We all grew up passing through all the stages in life, and constantly needing guidance from our mothers."

I studied Sih's face and saw that she was listening attentively.

I continued "If we found our own mothers stiff and unbending, we still tried to comply with their exigencies. However, we often had better guidance from some of our friends' mothers who had better approaches to bringing up a daughter. Now, consider me like a fairy godmother. A fairy godmother senses when everything is not right with the god daughter. You are my daughter's best friend and virtually my daughter too. That way I watch you as closely as I watch my daughter and a loving mother's instinct does not fail her. I

16

have noticed something in the air these last days which you prefer to keep between you and Titi. If it is something disturbing, I could help. If on the other hand it is something good, I could help you to make it better and lasting."

"Mum!" Titi protested.

I ignored Titi. I was observing Sih closely and was convinced that I had the bull by the horns. My words had not fallen on deaf ears.

"Auntie is right." she said to Titi "I wonder why I had not opened up to her all this while."

"That is it my girl." I said triumphantly. "Should we send Titi out and talk freely?"

"That is not necessary auntie." Sih said laughing. "She is into all my secrets and so far has been my best adviser."

"Well," I said "if you think so. Go ahead, include me into your secret and three heads will now make the best of it, three heads are better than two you know."

Titi relaxed. I saw quite some relief on her face.

"There is a young man who wants to marry me." Sih said.

"Marry you?" I asked "But that is wonderful. How is he? Handsome? Intelligent? Fun to be with? Respectful? Neat?"

Sih wavered, not seeming to know how to reply to my volley of questions. However, Titi had informed me that Sih was not actually hot for the guy so I was fast enough to change the approach.

"The qualities I have just mentioned are too much to ask of a prospective groom." I said. "At least, is he fun to be with?"

"I don't quite know him." Sih answered. "So there is no way I can determine that. However he is kind of uppity. When he came proposing, he was prancing around like a peacock, wonderfully sure of himself and looking at me as if he was certain that I should say 'yes' and rush into his dashed arms."

"From the way you describe him, you don't think much of him." I said. "So when he was proposing, there was no feet dragging, no gulping for words, no sighs?"

"None of that auntie." Sih said. "The bloke simply came to our house, sat on my father's favourite chair, helped himself greedily to my father's whisky placed in front of him by my aunt who had brought him, and asked to see me in a very commanding tone."

"And you responded to his command and made yourself available?" I asked.

"He asked me to sit in a chair with him and went directly into saying that he wanted to give me the pleasure of becoming his wife."

"Is that exactly what he said?" I asked shocked.

"That is just it." Sih replied. "He put it in a cruder and more repulsive manner; it is just that I don't quite remember the exact words."

"And what did you tell him?" I asked.

"I told him I was rather unprepared and needed time to reflect over his proposal."

"That was sharp of you." I congratulated, "And how did he take it?"

"He pressured me some but had to finally leave without a concrete answer."

"And your aunt?" I asked.

"She bludgeoned me with heavy statements on how my dullness could make me to lose the biggest marriage opportunity any girl could dream of. She urged me to act fast and accept the prospective suitor before he diverted his attention to some more deserving female."

"She said all that?" I asked. "Anyway, you said she is the one who had brought him along. How does she know him?"

"She was a classmate to his mother in school." Sih said

"Now, concerning this young suitor of yours who seems to be so full of himself, and that proposal of his, is that all that has been troubling you?" I asked.

"There is more. He comes from a rich family and it will appear my aunt scrounges there so often and understands that with me married to that guy, she would have opened a wide door through which she could have regular access to the wealth of that family."

"How greedy of her," I said pityingly. "And your mother? What does she think about it?"

"My mother does not want to openly oppose my aunt since she is my father's elder sister. Besides this guy has been insistent in his advances and has the full support of my aunt. My poor mother, who is now bombarded with accusations from my aunt on how she is the person that is misdirecting me, is also urging me to accept."

"And you?" I asked "What do you think? Do you see any way of ever loving this man?"

"Auntie, I cannot end up with such a pompous man as a husband." Sih answered.

"She is right mum," Titi said "Such men tend to be big lechers and even wife beaters. I won't want my friend to end up as a miserable wife. See the domineering way he approached her, even from the first time he came to propose."

"That bloke's approach may be crude," I said "But he may still sober down if Sih knows how to handle him. Men are not always what you take them to be. A quiet, respectful and hesitant suitor might instead turn out to be the lecher and

19

wife beater. Some of these men who grew up as lesser men and suddenly found themselves with wealth and power can become really unbearable. They suddenly find out that beautiful women are virtually at their beck and call whereas they used to be scared or too shy to approach these same women before. They now ignore the wife they could muster courage and get married to, now that they have easy access to other women they consider prettier and of a better class. Their legitimate wife becomes a bore to them."

"What a way of looking at it mum." Titi said.

"Always consider everything." I said. "On the other hand, these guys who act exaggeratedly macho may be covering up something. They may be handsome, well-to-do and exposed, but they don't have full confidence in themselves in front of a beautiful woman like you. They therefore put up such a show of confidence and always end up exaggerating."

"Mum," said Titi. "You are getting us confused."

"Not really." I said. "I simply want you to think well, consider all these options before you make a decision. Marriage is a sacred contract and should be considered seriously before entering into."

"Auntie," Sih said. "I have listened to you seriously. Now I want your advice. Do you think I should accept this guy?"

"That choice is yours to make my child." I said. "I have never seen or known him. From the way you describe him, he is certainly an odious young man. Whether he will make a good husband or not, I cannot tell but I think he is not the right man for you. You are still young, just out of your teens and other more deserving suitors will certainly come up. You have not even dated each other to permit you have the briefest idea about him apart from what your aunt says. Besides, from the way you present him I see no feeling of love, although to many, marriage does not solely depend on love."

I stood up and went to my bedroom, leaving the girls to talk over what I had just told them. I was sure I had handled the situation like an expert and this was confirmed to me shortly after Titi had seen off her friend and come back.

"Congrats mum." She said excitedly. "You were just great."

"Thank you." I said "I thought you were doing everything to prevent me from talking to your friend."

"I am sorry about that mum." She said. "But it is difficult for a daughter to trust her mum completely when it concerns things like this."

"Is that so?" I asked.

"I said I am sorry, but I must admit that you handled it like an expert. You should become a consultant to young girls who are facing the complications of accepting a husband. You should have seen how elated Sih was when you left us. I am lucky that I won't have to go and consult elsewhere when my time comes."

"Tell me," I said "was it just because of this issue that you girls spent weeks gossiping, conspiring and giggling?"

"That is a strong way of putting it mum." Titi said "But this bloke had been imposing his odious presence on Sih for all these weeks, encouraged by the greedy aunt who kept convincing the young man that she would find a way to convince or pressure Sih to accept him."

"And Sih reported to you on daily basis I suppose?" I said.

"It became our main form of entertainment. Each time the guy came and left, she made a beeline for this house and recounted everything. Together, we built up what she would tell the man the next time in order to ridicule him and send him away. Apparently, our cooked up responses were never strong enough because the guy kept coming back and hoping. But this time mum, you have spurred Sih into action. Thanks to you, she has developed a determination which she never thought she could muster. She is going to politely tell this man a clear 'no' next time he comes calling. No more beating about the bush."

"I only hope we are both right." I said. "In matters of love it is not easy to fit the right peg into the right hole."

My worry grew strong as Sih did not call around for close to two weeks. Titi did not seem to know why her friend was not calling and where she might have travelled to. All attempts by Titi to locate Sih were fruitless. My attempts to console Titi were taken kindly but I could see she still remained deeply worried. One day however, I came back to the house to a reception of happy girlish laughter and excited conversation. Sih had resurfaced and was having a hectic reunion with her bosom friend in the living room. Even the television was not switched on as usual as they seemed to be satisfied with the simple presence of each other. As soon as they noticed me, Sih jumped up, ran up to me and clung on my neck happily. I could immediately see that this was a young female with no troubles in the world.

"You are a wonderful fairy godmother." She was saying, smiling broadly "and you have made me a very happy woman. Thank you very much for your keen perception, timely intervention and wonderful advice."

"From this excited display of joy, I would imagine that everything worked out well." I said.

"It worked out perfectly Auntie." Sih said.

"You actually declared boldly that he was not your type and should go fetch for a bride somewhere else?" I asked

"I was quite determined but could not bring myself to say that."

She answered "I simply told him I was engaged to someone else."

"Golly," I said "who could have thought of that?" I suppose he went away with his tail between his legs."

"It was not that easy." She said "He accused me of being a jezebel, a hopeless good for nothing female clown, who led him along and deceived him to keep hoping whereas I was already hooked to some lousy jerk."

"That was very strong." I said.

"Devastating Auntie," replied Sih "and to make matters worse my aunt's reaction was quite extreme. She lashed out at me in no uncertain manner and even tried to get my dad to be severe on me."

"Shocking!" I said aghast. "Your mother still remained cautious?"

Women might tolerate a lot of rubbish and rough handling from in-laws, but rub their children the wrong way and you will be surprised.

"To avoid further trouble, my mother arranged in a hurry for me to go visit her sister in Bobong town." Sih said.

"How thoughtful of her." I said. "If that situation had continued, there would certainly have been a war in that house. But then a thought struck me suddenly. The level of happiness and excitement was much more than a simple rift with an unwanted suitor should have produced. I was sure there was something else.

"You still have more to tell me." I said conspiratorially.

"You see far auntie." She replied "Yes I have wonderful news for you. While in Bobong town I came across an old friend. He was actually the first boy I had ever gotten close to and we had dated for one year. But auntie, don't get me wrong. It was an innocent platonic relationship. I had enjoyed every moment I spent with him and he is really fun to be with. When he finally got a good job, he developed inside him a desire to make me his life partner but did not have the courage to say it. And then he got transferred to Bobong. We did not see each other for close to a year until that small holiday of mine, arranged to dispel trouble at home. I met him by chance in church when I went for Sunday mass, after which he invited me out. They say absence makes the heart grow fonder and I believe it is true."

"From the long separation between the two of you, he had missed you so much that he could muster the courage to propose to you I suppose?" I said.

"He went on his knees and begged me to become his wife."

"A marked difference from the pompous chap her aunt was trying to impose." Titi said softly.

"Yeah, a marked difference." I accepted. "And you certainly said 'yes' without thinking that you could act shy, hesitate a bit and pretend to accept reluctantly, the way your mothers used to do."

"We live in modern time auntie." Sih said. "When you like a man you don't need to pretend. Show him that his love for you is reciprocal and that you are equally eager to have him."

We all laughed in happiness.

"Thank you very much auntie." Sih said after a hearty laugh. I wish every girl could have the opportunity to consult you on these issues.

3

Ankunga

Ankunga was one of those women who always did what pleased them without stopping to think how other people were affected by their actions. We had known each other for a while and her husband, Chiabi Nchintoh was very close to Akoni. Chiabi and Akoni were so close that Chiabi often called on Akoni to complain about the escapades of his wife. I am sure Akoni knew as much about Ankunga's trespasses as her husband. But then Chiabi's complaints to Akoni were simply intended to empty his system of the pent up anguish that Ankunga caused him on very regular basis. Akoni had complained to me that each time he asked Chiabi whether he should tick off Ankunga for her loose ways, Chiabi would plead with him not to go provoking his dear wife with rude accusations.

In our circles, we thought Ankunga was taking things to extremes. We all belonged to a club where the emancipation and empowerment of the woman was our key objective but we knew our limits. A man can be quite gentle, respectful and understanding, just like a child, but push him to the wall and you may end up receiving a few surprise jabs on the face, or a declaration of the intention to bring in another woman. Act within a reasonable range and you would get much understanding, even from some macho men.

However, whenever we tried to tamper down Ankunga's exuberances, her reply was always the same. Her belief was that, you should be extremely hard on a man; otherwise he would want to drag you by the nose and trample upon your every God given right.

After sacrificing much of his time almost every day listening to the sombre complaints of Chiabi about his wife's misdemeanours, Akoni finally decided he had to do something about it. He was up to his tether with his friend's marital problems. That night while we were in our bedroom, chatting away like the happy couple we were, sharing jokes and exciting titbits we had gathered during the day, Akoni suddenly became serious.

"What is it dear?" I asked a bit worried.

"This issue of Chiabi and Ankunga," he said. "It has gone too far. We must put a stop to it."

"How can we dear?" I asked "They are the ones who know and understand best their relationship. Where do we come in?"

"It is clear that Chiabi cannot be man enough to handle his wife's excesses." Akoni said. "She is taking advantage of this weakness and making my friend's life miserable."

"Wait a minute." I said. "Your friend loves his wife fondly and that is it. They have adjusted their life to suit them. He is certainly peace loving and does not want to become confrontational."

"You are just saying that because you are a woman." Akoni said. "All of you are aware of the rough treatment Chiabi gets from his wife. He is like putty in her hands, for Christ's sake."

"That is true," I admitted, "but maybe he enjoys it that way. I saw in some sex magazines where during sex, some men prefer to leave the active male role to the woman. Some even ask the women to horsewhip them, an act of total domination by the woman and total submission by the man."

"Those are perverts" Akoni said "especially those that have to be tied up and horsewhipped by their sex partner before they can have an erection."

"That does not cancel out the fact that many men prefer to leave the leadership role to their wives." I said.

"I cannot argue that." Akoni said "I agree with you that there are some men who prefer the role of the woman and some women who prefer the role of the man."

"Anyway," I said "a family is a family and any of the partners could be strong willed, overbearing or have initiative, meanwhile the other partner simply follows. Mind you it could be the woman who always takes the initiative and leads on."

"The man is understood to be the head of the family and the leader if it comes to that." Akoni said "You women are known as the gentle sex to show that your role is secondary or passive. You can't imagine a man always waiting for the woman to take the initiative and obeying her orders like a faithful dog. They call females the weaker sex because they need to be protected, defended and assisted when it comes to tedious work or tough things."

I could not help laughing. A woman must defend the sex when confronted with a male but we are aware of the fact that some of us do exaggerate a wee bit.

"This is not a laughing matter." Akoni said. "I suggest you speak to your friend. Make her see reason."

I simply smiled back.

"Why can she not be like you?" He added flatteringly.

"What do I tell her?" I asked. "I rather think you should advise your friend on how to manage his marital situation and live as happily as you do."

"No dear." He said. "You must admit that the real problem is Ankunga. Her waywardness is not a secret to any of us."

"We could equally say," I replied "that the real problem is Chiabi. He should learn how to dialogue with his wife, make her see and accept her faults and help her to correct them. You don't correct an errant wife by beating her to a pulp or lashing out with a sharp tongue. But then, you cannot make a woman responsible by being docile and receptive to all her defaults."

Finally I decided to do something. I thought I should look for just that moment when Ankunga's husband would be out of the house. That would enable us have a womanly talk uninterrupted.

I called on her the next day and was happy to see that her husband was not at home. We could talk freely woman to woman. But then I had to introduce the topic carefully and watch out so I don't say something revolting to her and curb her willingness to listen.

"Welcome to my humble home." She said. "What beer should I offer you, or would you like some whiskey or gin?"

Another woman would have offered me a juice or soft drink. In Kenya or in some of those parts of the world where tea is a popular form of entertainment among women, I would have been offered tea. But my friend here specified the stuff she normally liked, probably an indication that if men offered their visiting friends whiskey, we women should be capable of doing the same.

"None of that." I said. "A glass of water would do."

"Mineral water drinkers." She said with disgust. "That is what keeps us several steps behind the men."

She brought me a glass of fruit juice from the refrigerator and opened a beer for herself.

"Thank you." I said, accepting the drink. I was groping for the best way to bring up what I had come to say so I did not want to insist on the glass of water I had asked for.

"Some men too drink mineral water you know." I said carefully.

"Yes," she replied. "Those men who are sick."

I laughed at this.

"Well, you know when it comes to alcohol God has made us weaker than men." I said.

"I can beat a man any time." She said boastfully. "My husband is no match for me."

I saw an opportunity here and took it.

"Talking about your husband," I said "don't you think you are too hard on him?"

"Hard?" She asked. "How?"

"It is popular knowledge that in this household you are rather the man and he is the woman."

"Are your rumour mongers trying to say that in a home a man should have more rights than a woman?" she asked

"Not quite that, but nature, culture and society have made us women to grow up accepting certain norms."

"Like what?" She asked curtly

"We all accept that the man is the head of the family. When we get married to him, we adopt his name just as you have done. You are called Mrs. Nchintoh. In ancient Europe women even called their husbands, Lords. In many parts of Africa, we give them special respect. In Komland in Cameroon, we offer them the gizzard of every chicken we cook which is a show of great respect. In other parts of the country, women stoop or kowtow in front of the men when

31

offering them food or water to wash their hands before eating."

Ankunga burst into laughter of ridicule. I decided to give her enough time to laugh before continuing but suddenly she stopped laughing and said.

"If you misguided females are afraid of the men folk, then it is your cup of tea."

"We are not afraid of them." I said patiently. "We give them respect, same as we expect much respect from them. Are you not flattered when a man pulls a chair for you to sit, or opens the car door for you, or appreciates your dress, hairstyle or perfume?"

"That is all empty flattery." Ankunga said "When a man does that to you, he knows what he wants."

She sipped her beer.

"A woman's relationship with a man depends on how the relationship started." She said. "If he approaches you like a dictator and a bully and you have the folly of accepting his advances, then your relationship will continue like that for ever. You will remain a slave and possibly an object on which he regularly vents his anger through battery."

I simply shook my head and listened.

"If he approaches you like a sweet talking Casanova, using lots of charm but without any dime in his pockets, and you accept him as he is and proceed to foot his lavish bills, you will continue like that in marriage, paying all his bills and wallowing in his empty charms. If on the other hand, he approaches you like a trembling leaf, unsure of himself and places himself at your beck and call, then that is how your marriage life will be. My husband falls in this last category and I intend to keep it like that."

I saw that the situation needed a lot of tact.

"Maybe you are right" I said. "But then, you could limit this commanding spirit over your husband to your home. Why make it public? Everyone is talking about it."

"I don't care what people say." she replied.

"You should." I replied firmly. "If you love your husband, you should not do things that hurt him. If you don't care what people say, he does care."

I noticed that Akunga was thoughtful.

"And then," I said "you openly go out with other men. That is the biggest disrespect you can ever give any husband."

She jumped back like a tigress.

"Men do it every day! They abandon their wives at home, and have affairs with every woman that accepts their advances. They hang out with secretaries and even house girls. Some of us who have the opportunity should retaliate on behalf of women."

"That is not correct." I said heatedly. "When you have an affair with another man you are not only hurting or disrespecting your husband. You are also hurting another sister whose husband or fiancé you might be sleeping with. How would you feel if you found your husband cheating? Besides your husband is a good and respectable man. He is known for his impeccable lifestyle and you cannot punish him by retaliating on behalf of women who would rather be annoyed if they knew what you were doing."

I examined Akunga's face to see whether there was any reaction to what I was saying. Her countenance was bland.

I continued.

"You see, we women are not as weak and docile as you think. You need to see what transpires in the bedroom behind locked doors. I tell my husband my mind and handle him quite roughly for any transgression during the day. No man wants to be openly challenged or scolded by a woman. Even the children would not want to see that. Would you or your mother want to see your brother's wife disgracing him in public?"

She shook her head.

"Besides," I continued. "Push a man to the wall and he will revolt, and when that happens he goes right to the other extreme. It has been known to happen often. The scales fall from their eyes they generally say and they realize that they had been fools all the time. Then they want to buy back lost time."

Ankunga stirred uncomfortably. I did not relent.

"You may not have realized it but the respect our husbands get in public rubs off to us." I said. "If your husband is president, you become the first lady and it goes with all the respect. Some women like Oprah have gained a lot of respect through their own efforts but you would agree with me that many more have gained respect through their husband's positions. That is why in public we promote respect for our husbands. You in your case are rather destroying the little respect that your husband can muster."

Akunga sighed.

"If you have noticed, Muslim women give their husbands much respect, especially in public." I followed up. "They are even willing to wear ugly veils despite the fact that it hides their beauty, just because they want their husbands to be respected by all."

Ankunga sighed again.

"And remember," I said "that in our tribes women celebrate the coming of a child in what they call *born house*. During these occasions, women loosen up and do quite obscene things through songs and dances that any decent woman would not perform in the presence of her husband and his friends. Yet, the songs all insinuate the dominant role of the man, his sexual prowess and his important place in the life of the woman."

This time, Ankunga actually smiled.

"Marriage life means challenging each other only for the good." I continued encouraged. "Don't cheat on your husband only because you want revenge or you suspect that he is going out with other women. Instead, a woman is supposed to exploit her womanhood fully and even bring back the flame in expired husbands. Don't fill yourself with alcohol simply because you want to challenge your husband's drinking habits and don't stay out late because your husband stays out late with the boys once in a while. Be yourself."

"Okay, I have heard it all." Akunga said "Let me take time and think it over."

"You are not taking any time" I said insistently. "You will jump to the kitchen and prepare the food Mr. Nchintoh likes best. Then show him love and respect immediately he comes back home."

"Are you sure you are not pushing me to become a slave to him? Men can take advantage of any situation." She said.

"Not your husband. I rather think that he would become quite a happy man. We all show our husbands lots of respect and love but we have our limits and they respect it. In many homes, the women make main decisions but from behind so that it does not become like an argument or competition."

I left Ankunga, convinced that my mission was a success.

That evening as we lay in bed, Akoni was eager to know what had transpired between Akunga and myself and whether I had succeeded in getting her to see her husband as a worthy spouse and head of the family.

"The situation is really complicated." I said. "But I think I did my best."

"There is something wrong with that friend of yours." Akoni said. "She is one of those females that regret their sex. Why is it that many women would have preferred to be men?"

"That is not true." I said rather angrily. "Women are proud of their womanhood and feminism. That is why their gait, their dressing, their fragrances and tastes are always subtle and exquisite, not as crude as male stuff."

"And all this is for our attention." Akoni said.

"Of course." I said. "You want to keep your man loving you and always attracted to you."

"Although you might end up attracting the attention of other men?" Akoni smiled roguishly.

I let that go.

"That is where you have a real woman." I said. "She is attractive and simple but knows how to say 'no' to other men."

"Bravo!" Akoni said, "But that does not cancel out the fact that some women would have loved to be men instead. One of the most popular female artists sang something about what she would do if she were a boy."

"How many women go in for sex change?" I asked. "Many men are getting themselves transformed into women. Then you have the ladyboys of Thailand, transsexuals in France and the beautiful Brazilian Shemales with massive cocks, and full and well-rounded breasts. All these take hormones to get transformed to look like women, after which they dress like women and get picked up like whores. You tell me." I said smiling. "Is it women who want to be men or men who want to be women?"

36

Akoni was beaten and admitted it by dropping the topic.

"We seem to have strayed completely from our main point of discussion." Akoni said. "How did it go with Ankunga?"

"I used all the tact I could muster and I am sure we will get positive results." I replied. "All we need to do now is sit back and wait for your friend to tell us tomorrow."

"Thanks dear." Akoni said appreciatively. "You would have brought happiness back into my friend's life if this works."

For a whole week, Akoni did not receive any complaints from Chiabi. Chiabi had not even called to see him as usual.

"I wonder what has become of Chiabi." Akoni said as we sat in the living room conversing.

"He has not come complaining to you about his wife's escapades?" I asked. "Or inform you about any positive change in her since I last talked to her?"

"Not at all and that is strange." replied Akoni "Besides, Chiabi never spends more than two days without calling on me."

"You had better check on him then." I advised "He could be ill. Besides, we need to know the results off my encounter with Ankunga."

"This is weekend" Akoni said, "and we don't have work. Let's go and visit Chiabi and his wife."

"That would be a good idea." I said. "I would like to see how my friend Ankunga is doing."

We jumped into the car and drove to the Nchintoh's imagining that we may either find Chiabi in bed with fever or find him cowering in front of a haranguing Ankunga.

We were surprised at what we found. Chiabi was reclining on a couch in the sitting room and Ankunga was ensconced in a chair by his side. What was interesting about it all was that they were chatting away happily like two very close sweethearts. As we came in Ankunga stood up to offer us seats. Before, she would have expected Chiabi to do this. After ensuring that we were comfortably seated, she moved back to Chiabi and rubbing his chest, cooed fondly into his ear.

"Would you want me to get you something my darling?"

"Bring a bottle of Jack Daniels and some ice for Akoni and I." Chiabi replied "Maybe Mawumi will prefer some juice as usual."

As Akunga went to get glasses and something for us to drink, I pinched Akoni on the lap.

"You have been out of circulation" Akoni said to Chiabi.

"Akunga and I had some kind of a marriage renewal" Chaibi said smiling happily. "This past week we have been having a real honeymoon, I don't know what suddenly came over her, but she simply changed like a chameleon. Since it was for the best, I tagged along and we have been having a swell time. I wish life had been like this all along."

I was wondering whether I should tell him that I was the shadow behind his bliss when Ankunga bustled in with our drinks.

"Dear," she said to Chiabi "you owe a basket of thanks to my friend here. Mawumi is the best consultant I would recommend for wives.

4

Titi

"**M**um, there is this book that my friend gave me to read." Titi shouted excitedly as she came into my bedroom.

"Is it?" I asked. "Why does your friend think that it is a good book?"

"I don't know yet." She confessed. "She gave it to me to read, recommending that it is good for girls who have just attained the age when they could get married and where the choice of a good husband might have to be considered seriously."

"In that case," I said "I shall have to read it first and decide whether it is okay for you to read."

"But mum!" Titi protested. "My friend Sih has read it and recommends it too, so I think it is okay."

"All the same," I said firmly. "I shall read it first and see whether it is good material for you. Falling in love and getting married is not guided by novels. It is true judgment, patience and other criteria that you need."

I kept the book away in a drawer and ushered her out of the room.

"Now, go and do your homework." I advised. "I will prepare a nice meal."

My husband Akoni had travelled out of town that morning to be back the next day.

My intention was to stay up in bed that night and acquaint myself with the contents of the book Titi had brought home. I took a cup of Kola coffee after the meal to help keep me awake. I pulled the book out of the drawer, adjusted my pillows and lay back to read. The author of the book was Vanpukerhoff. What a name, I thought, already disliking the book. I dug into the story.

A certain Boozinsky had this female friend, a university mate called Natalia. He thought he was seriously in love with her and tried on several occasions to pass through this burning feeling for her. She was always smiling and caring but showed no sign of any sexual attachment. At one point he complained to a friend and both of them concluded that she could be a lesbian, and they were right. Boozinsky eventually discovered that while he was struggling to get Natalia to accept him as a lover, she was rather concentrating on another female student for whom she had developed real sexual love. The irony there was that this other female student was heterosexual and had openly showed Boozinsky in so many ways that she had fallen for him and all he needed to do was to approach. Disgusted with the whole situation, Boozinsky had given up pursuing Natalia for her love and travelled to far off lands. His ardour for Natalia still lingered however and he kept track of her activities. She became a very successful lawyer and eventually got married to some other female, and in this marriage she played the role of the dominant male. She was now married to a wife thus obliterating Boozinsky's chances of ever getting married to her. One day Boozinsky was dragged to court for a felony he had not actually committed. Everything however pointed against him until at the last moment Natalia learnt of the situation stepped in like a good friend, defended him like the astute lawyer she was and set him free. During a small reception afterwards, all the love Boozinsky had for Natalia bubbled over and he went up to her and embraced her warmly. Holding Natalia's hands fondly and looking into her face with lots of love, he declared that he had remained single because of his love for her. He said he was aware that his open declaration of love might hurt Natalia's wife but said Natalia's wife had nothing to fear because he did not intend to become a wife. Rather, he wanted to be Natalia's husband.

I dropped the book in disgust. No way. My daughter could not be allowed to read things like this.

If you are heterosexual, look for your heterosexual woman and marry. You cannot make yourself happy by wasting your love on a woman who can feel nothing but platonic love for you.

I dosed off into a worried sleep. There are certain things that are to be handled with the utmost care, like determining whether your child is gay, and learning how to handle it. In America and Europe it might be easier but back here in Africa it is still a very delicate subject.

The next morning Titi was knocking on my bedroom door.

"Mum, can I have the book now?" she called from outside.

"You may," I replied "but you cannot read it."

"Ow mum," she protested again "what could be wrong with reading a simple book?"

"Because it is not the type of book you should read." I said sternly. "I will give you the book, but you will take it back straight to your friend and tell her your mother frowns on such literature."

"Why mother, is it pornographic?" Titi asked.

"I won't say that," I replied, "but the book is not good for you. Have you dressed up to go to school?"

"Yes mum, I should be off now" she said.

41

"Have you had something to eat?"

"Yes mum." She replied. "Are you not going out today?"

"I am feeling a bit tired but I will be up and out soon." I said. "Now run along and hand that book back."

Titi took off.

When she came back that evening I wanted to be sure that she had handed over the book. Titi was quite honest and obedient but one can never be too sure with girls who were just leaving their teens.

"You have given the book back I hope", I asked.

"Yes, I handed it back immediately I got to school."

"And you did not attempt to see what was in it?" I asked.

"I was sorely tempted," she admitted "but all I know about the book is the little my friend told me."

"What did she tell you?" I asked concerned.

"Oh not much really." Titi said.

"Tell me, I want to hear." I said.

"But you read it yourself mum!" Titi replied.

"I want to hear what she told you." I repeated insistently.

"Well, she said it was the story of some fellow who was in love with a lesbian. The love was not reciprocated because she was rather in love with another woman, and this other woman was strongly attracted to the man. Some kind of a vicious circle."

"You see why I told you the book was not good?" I asked.

"I don't know," she said "but I thought lesbians only get attracted to lesbians."

"How would you know if you are not one?" I asked.

"How does one know that she is a lesbian mum?" Titi asked.

I was confused, fogged. Truly I had no answer to the question. I could not start encouraging my young daughter to like men and it is mainly when a woman prefers men that you can figure out she is not a complete lesbian.

"How do you feel about men?" I finally asked cautiously.

"How should I feel about them?" she asked "Men are just men, at times fun to be with but often boring. I prefer the company of my girlfriends."

I panicked a little. "At your age," I said "a girl could have a date, a boy of course" I said with emphasis.

"Ah that mum," she said "there are always boys vying to take me out on dates."

"And you often refuse or accept?" I was panicking again, but this time the reason was different.

My daughter comforted me by her next statement.

"Mama, rest assured that you have a good daughter. You have done everything to bring me up like a good girl. I won't let you down."

"Thank God." I thought.

That evening when I recounted everything to Akoni he simply smiled.

"You women often overwork yourselves and worry over nothing when it concerns your daughters." He said.

"That may be your opinion" I said "but that is because we try to avoid extremes. Men either spoil their daughters or turn out to be too severe on them."

After some brief silence Akoni smiled again and asked me.

"Would you prefer that your daughter turns out a lesbian who respects herself and has one or two dates, or you would rather prefer that she grows up oversexed or an outright nymphomaniac?"

"I refuse to answer that question." I said.

"It is because deep inside you there is an inhibition against lesbians. What if you had been born like that?"

That night I thought seriously about my husband's statement. What indeed if I had been born homosexual?

The next day I was one of the guest speakers in one of the popular girl schools in town. There were four guest speakers, a stout middle aged fellow and three women. The speaker just before me had as topic for her paper 'Lesbianism: A disease worse than AIDS'. She handled her topic like a road compactor engaged in levelling any possible bump on the road surface. She harangued the little girls as if they were all confirmed lesbians and warned them severely to beware of any female who had such tendencies. She gave no room for possibilities of being born like that and insisted that it was practiced by women who did not know their right from their left. She used religion to further strengthen her arguments.

When I came up as the next speaker, I was happy that I had already been prepared by my husband's question the previous evening.

I decided to start with the topic on homosexuality and broached it with the utmost care.

"I would like to start by touching a bit on the topic of homosexuality." I said. "In Europe, it is quite common. Here in Africa, it exists but still has some strong stigma attached to it. Every mother wants her daughter to grow up a heterosexual, who would get married and produce grandchildren. On the other hand, none of them wants this heterosexual daughter to be oversexed or a nymphomaniac. Some people however believe that homosexuality is a natural trait just like nymphomania or kleptomania. It is true there

44

are a few adventurers among homosexuals who simply go in for the sake of trying. What I think we should all understand is that it is only a true homosexual who understands what he or she sees or enjoys in a person of the same sex, whereas nature had designed a situation where members of the opposite sex should be attracted to each other. But to bitterly condemn homosexuality and paint homosexuals to look like demons is completely wrong."

I looked around the hall. The girls were silent and attentive. It was difficult to deduce whether the girls totally disagreed with what I was saying or were very interested.

"Don't get me wrong." I said "I am not advising you to go out and start practicing lesbianism. Homosexuality is not something you go experimenting with. You are still too young to get involved with sex and not old enough to determine whether you have homosexual tendencies. Persons, who consider themselves as straight, look at homosexuality as a problem but many homosexuals don't see it as a problem and simply consider it as a sexual option. The real problem is the stigma, for it pushes many homosexuals into shying away from openly declaring their sexual tendencies, while it makes others to hate themselves for being that way. My advice to you is that you are still young and have your studies in front of you. Forget about sex till you come of age and you will not have to worry about homosexuality."

I suddenly remembered something important.

"But don't forget," I continued "that you are in a girl's school and once in a while you may have a teacher or any member of staff who does not understand that you are still children and tries to take advantage of you to satisfy their lust. Don't fall for such moves as you are not ripe enough for sex. Resist and report them to the authorities if possible. Don't allow your young tender bodies to be defiled."

The rest of my talk was not followed as keenly as this first part but I was sure I was rated highest among the speakers by the girls. The principal of the school even gave me a hearty handshake at the end, congratulating me for a brilliant presentation. We were ushered into an adjoining room for snacks.

At the end of the occasion I packed my things and went out to my car, and was surprised to find several girls waiting for me. I smiled at them and stood to hear what they wanted.

"Are you a lesbian?" one of them asked.

"No!" I said "I am married to a man I love and we have children.

"You defended homosexuality so wonderfully" another girl said "We thought you were one."

"That is okay" I said. "You don't have to be a homosexual before you make people understand that it is a situation that you have to live with if you have such tendencies. Homosexuality is not a disease for which you can simply take medicine and cure. But why are you girl's particular about my opinion on homosexuality?"

"This is a single girl's school and at times we have certain desires" one of the girls said. "We end up toying with each other but still do not quite understand whether we are actual lesbians or we are just taking off steam. After all some of our brothers tell us that in boys' schools they do the same"

"If you want my advice," I said, all of you are still too young to think of things like that. If you have any urges, suppress them. Wait till when you will be old enough to get married. When young men start asking for your hand, you will be able to determine whether you love hooking up with the opposite sex or your desires are only for members of your sex."

"Thank you auntie" they said.

As I was getting into my car I heard a voice from behind.

"Hey, you woman from Sodom or is it Gomorrah?" the voice said "I hope you were not imparting your homosexuality on those little girls. I know your type and wish God could strike all of you off the earth."

I turned around to look. It was the female who had blasted homosexuality to no end, probably angry that I had softened up her torrent of venom against lesbians.

"Hello," I said "Has a homosexual jilted or raped you before? Your anger against them seems to be based on something terrible."

"I already complained to the school authorities" she said "and warned them to watch out for you. The likes of you should not be allowed around vulnerable girls like these. European priests are often accused of sodomy against little mass boys, but I am sure they come nowhere near you."

I entered my car and drove off.

Sodom and Gomorrah, I thought and smiled. If right back in those Biblical days homosexuality was common, then you cannot be too hard on them today. Although it is considered by many as a sin, is it actually a crime? Should it be banned like some countries have done?

Two days later, while sitting in my office and wondering about the issue of freewill supposed to have been given to all of us by God, a sudden phone call made me to start. I picked up the phone and declared myself available.

"Is that Mrs. Mawumi Ngongnuwi on the line?" A male voice asked from the other end.

"Yes." I answered

"Your talk in that girls' school the other day was quite interesting." the unknown person said.

"Thank you." I said wondering who could be on the line. "How did you get to hear about it? I thought I was simply talking to school girls."

"You were," the voice said "but there were a few of us organizers in the background."

"I see." was all I could say.

"Your husband, Akoni Ngongnuwi is a friend and a class mate and has been covered by us too. Everything we do is filmed."

"Who are you really?" I asked.

"Our organization strives to promote good practices in society. We also tackle social prejudices. If you check on the invitation you received the other time, you will see the name of our organization and address. If you have disposed of it already, another one for this new occasion is coming this afternoon. I just wanted to inform you before the formal invitation arrives."

"What do you want me to talk on this time" I asked.

"We are coming right to your office to discuss it." the voice said "Or at what time would you prefer us to come?"

I looked at my watch it was 1pm

"Come right away," I said "but make sure this time you don't pair me up with speakers that are easily hurt and cannot resist hurling abuses at others."

"We are on our way madam." the voice said, ignoring the last part of my statement.

Thirty minutes later, they were ushered into my office and I immediately remembered seeing them at the school. The person who had been speaking to me looked very athletic and likable. The other was a female who equally looked bright and quite attractive.

"Mrs. Ngongnuwi," the male visitor said "we are sorry to have interrupted your work at such short notice."

I was later to learn that he was called Nchoji and the lady was Ngoin.

"That seems to be your mode of operating." I replied without any animosity. "Last time you sent me an invitation to talk just one day before the event, without giving me enough time to prepare."

"We are sorry about that" Nchoji said

"Why have you come yourself this time?" I asked. "Last time you simply sent me the invitation."

"This one is kind of delicate." Ngoin said. "It is something we need to present to you first so that you see whether you can handle it."

"Do I have any option to reject or accept it?" I asked.

Nchoji and Ngoin laughed.

"Did I ask a funny question?" I asked

"We are sorry for that." Nchoji said. "However, you know very well that we are depending on you because of your talent. You have the choice to refuse or accept of course, but would you reject such an effort to save females from dire situations?"

He had pricked my soft spot. I am no fanatical feminist, but will stand up for a fellow woman anytime.

"What do you expect me to do?" I asked.

"Many of the old retired senior workers in this town are members of the Anlahsi Club". He said

I knew the Anlahsi Club very well, a club to which everybody who claimed to be of a certain class in society strived to become a member. My husband and some of his friends where members and many of the other members were old illustrious citizens now retired from active duty. Without much to do in an office and with much leisure time in their hands these old fellows normally hung around the club, swam, played snookers, chess, draughts or simply drank and chatted.

"Yes." I said. "What about the old geezers? Do they suddenly want to become young?"

"In a way." Ngoin said

"The point is," Nchodji cut in. "These old fellows used to be respectable old men, faithful to their wives and retired in every aspect."

"What do you mean by retired in every aspect?" I asked.

"Because of their advanced ages," said Ngoin "they were sexually tired and could no longer run around like small boys."

"That is understood." I said. "What is wrong with that?"

"Some very effective Chinese products have been introduced to them that enhances sexual performance."

"Why don't these Chinese allow natural processes to take their course?" I asked.

"This product has considerably revived the sexual prowess in these old men and they no longer want to see anything in skirts pass without trying it."

"This Chinese product is some sort of Viagra I suppose," I said. "So what is the problem?"

"There would have been no problem if these horny old men stuck to their wives." Ngoin said.

"The problem is actually two fold." Nchoji said "These old chaps would not spare any female they can lay hands on. Friends of their wives, babysitters and house girls, their daughters' friends, and even their own daughters and granddaughters are all vulnerable. They often have their way because they generally have much cash to throw around. The other part to it is that most of them would not even use the condom."

I felt horrified.

"Such lechers should be put away." I said.

"By whom?" Nchodji asked. "God had designed a natural way of Curbing the sexual desires of old men by naturally reducing their stamina and sexual capacities at old age. Powerful drugs have now come to counter all this and a horny old man is far more dangerous than a horny young man or teenager."

"Such products should be banned." I said.

"Who will ban them?" Ngoin asked, "Most of the big lawmakers are men of a certain age and need these things to function."

"So," I said. "Where do I come in?"

"We have organized a sensitization session to be held at Anlahsi Club on Saturday." Nchoji said, "All the speakers shall be well selected women like you."

"And what do we say to them?" I asked.

"What we want from this is to make them feel guilty and adjust, without necessarily shouting or abusing them." Ngoin said "If they cannot completely abstain, at least we want them to use the condom."

Given the circumstances I was obliged to accept. That night, I received some encouragement from Akoni who told me that old men may leer at me during my talk but they don't bite.

"But be careful." he added. "From what I hear, these old chaps will certainly attempt to chat you up."

"Let them try," I said vehemently.

"That is not the spirit." Akoni said "You are supposed to be tactfully convincing them to give up sexual excesses. A blunt or angry rejection of their advances may rather hurt and push them to refuse to listen to you."

"Are old men so complicated?" I asked

"There are old men of all categories." Akoni said. "You have the old playboys who from childhood were ladykillers. You have some that were just normal and grew up just like that. The worst among them are those that grew up as shy men or men who were afraid of approaching women because of one complex or another. At a certain age they discover almost too late that a woman is just a woman and all a man needs to do is to chat her up or throw a bit of cash around. Some parvenu's too suddenly find themselves capable of paying for a woman's love and go mad.

"I did not know there was so much to this." I said.

"Much more." Akoni said "There are many men who grew up sexually weak and remained docile. Suddenly they come across one product or another that enhances their sexual capacity and makes them supermen. Such persons always want to catch up".

I had enough time to think over the whole thing and prepare well for the meeting with the old chaps.

I was quite shocked to discover that I had been placed as the first speaker. I had thought I would observe others first and use the reaction of the old men to adjust and polish my strategy. I decided to start from the angle of the use of condoms before coming round to abstention. Summoning enough courage, I took the rostrum and plunged ahead. I was already thinking that I had been apprehensive for nothing and the old men were docile respectable folk when without warning, I was rudely interrupted by one of the old goats.

"Excuse me madam," he said "you are saying that if you allow me to go into that juicy thing that you certainly have, I should sheath my old Johnny with some lousy rubber glove?"

I stood there embarrassed while the old men chuckled happily. The fellow who had asked the question remained seriously waiting for an answer.

"Only your wife should allow you to enter her without protection." I said "And understand that here, I am simply giving you a lecture and can never be at your disposal otherwise."

"What does a man enjoy if he is blocked away from the juicy parts by a bloody rubber?" the old man continued stubbornly.

"He remains protected." I said. "And if there is nothing to enjoy that way, he should not bother to try it."

"Madam," another bloke said. "I no longer have long to live and God made this thing for us to enjoy. How do you enjoy by protecting the enjoyment with rubber?"

"There are many other ways through which you can enjoy the rest of your lives safely without necessarily thinking about sex.", I said. "You just need to make up your minds. You could limit yourself to enjoying a game, watching TV, reading good books or having a small drink, or just chatting with your wife."

"That is just the problem." said an old fellow with snow white hair. "When we were younger, we could smoke, drink, enjoy good and exotic food or engage in exertive sports; but now doctors have blocked us from all these. As for our old wives, they may bustle around and do many things for us as if we were babies but they no longer make interesting company. How else do we enjoy these last days of ours on Earth if we don't exploit all available sources?"

"If you are talking about sexual satisfaction," I said. "Your wife is there and will always comply if you are gentle and understanding. If your wife is dead, marry another woman and be faithful to her."

"But young women strongly want old people like us." said another old fellow. "You need to see the way they move their buttocks provocatively in front of us."

"That is your sordid imagination." I said. "What does a pretty little girl or young woman see in a wrinkled old man apart from the opportunity to make cheap money? In your distorted minds you imagine that every woman who passes by, is trying to attract your attention whereas their movements are innocent."

"Talking about condoms," said a smart looking man. "We risk the possibility of losing a hard erection if we waste time trying to put one on and that is why we dive in as soon as we have managed to have a hard on."

"Give up each time it droops." I advised.

"Young lady," an old coot said. "All what you have been saying about condoms is theory but we were taught in school that practical demonstrations are better to make even the dullest student to understand. You and I could do it practically so that your lesson is complete and we all learn how to wear the condom and use it."

For this sensitization exercise, we had been provided wooden phalluses to use for demonstrations but I had refused it. It was certain, I had argued that all the participants must have used a condom at one time or another in their sex lives. Their rejection of it now was based on laziness, fear that they may lose the erection in the process of wearing the condom or the desire to enjoy sex directly. The idea behind the exercise as I understood was mainly to convince the old blokes to abstain or to continue using condoms.

"Who in this room has never used a condom?" I asked.

There was no response.

"I take it, all of you have used condoms," I said. "Either with your wives or when cheating on your wives?"

"That is not the way to put it." The bald lecher said. "You don't expect an old man to admit in front of all of us that he has never used a condom. Let's just do the practical thing."

"Who wants to use condoms with his own wife anyway?" One of them asked. "Does your husband use condoms with you?"

"There might be unsafe periods," I explained "during which a couple may want to have sex but are not interested in making children at that time."

"You are digressing from the aspect of a practical demonstration." The bald old man insisted

I ignored the fool.

"It is quite clear," I said for all to hear "that everybody present has used a condom before. My role here is to convince and encourage you to continue to use it if you must live a frivolous lifestyle. I am certain that your wives still want their sex lives fulfilled. Stick to them."

I now turned to the coot who had been insisting on a practical demonstration.

"Since you want a practical demonstration," I said, "we shall have one."

The bloke leered at me.

"Our demonstration shall be on abstinence." I said.

"That is absurd." He said angrily. "What kind of demonstration could be on abstinence? Abstinence means doing nothing and you can't demonstrate doing nothing."

"Abstinence means avoiding sexual intercourse," I said "or resisting certain urges or rejecting sexual advances from old lechers like you."

"Let's see the demonstration." One of the men said chuckling.

"Act one " I said "I am soliciting and you are rejecting me out right, telling me that you are fine with your wife in the house."

"And act two?"

"You ask me to go out with you and I refuse," I said "and tell you respectfully that you should go home to your wife. You then regret why you went in for such disgrace when your good wife is there at home."

"Is that all?" the coot asked. "What is the use acting such a thing?" he said "Let's give it up."

I continued to the end of my talk without further interruption.

At the end, I heard myself being described by some of the old men as a tough woman.

That night at home I finished my meal and asked Titi to brew me some tea.

"Titi," I said as she brought my tea "That book of yours has led to many things."

"You discovered in the end that it was a good book?" she asked.

"Not that," I said hastily. "I am tired now anyway, we shall discuss it tomorrow."

The next day something else came up that made me forget about every other thing. I had been quite busy at work and left for home tired when it was closing time. The trip back home made things worse as some unnecessary traffic jam compelled me to spend much more time than usual to get home. When I finally got there, I was only thinking of a warm bath, a meal and my bed. As I stepped into the house, my daughter Titi was waiting for me.

"Mum," she said without any preamble "I think I am falling in love."

The statement took me by surprise. She was barely twenty years of age, tender and quite innocent. I looked at her childlike face, frightened by what she had just said.

"But you can't be falling in love." I said hotly. "You are still a child and still have your education in front of you."

"Mum, I am already an adult." she replied. "I am twenty and I am already in university. Does that not make me old enough to fall in love?"

"What do you know about love?" I asked. "You have had a few innocent dates with one or two of your school mates that I know of but you have never mentioned anything about love before. You are getting me frightened."

"It is because this time it is different." She said I really have this feeling for the guy."

"What is his name?" I asked

"Tangnangkoli" she said

The name sounded a bit odd but I let it go.

"How did the relationship start? I asked.

"It has not yet started" she said. "He has not asked me out."

"That does not make sense" I said.

"Mum," she said "you have to understand. Although I have this strong feeling for him and terribly want to be with him, I cannot simply walk up to him and tell him that I love him."

I understood what my daughter was going through quite well. In virtually all cultures and communities on earth, it is the man who proposes to the woman so he has the possibility of making his choice. When they talk about equal opportunity in this world, it is all misleading. A man looks for the woman that he thinks he likes and proposes marriage, but a woman is condemned to accept the offer that comes. A woman may see a man of her choice but can only have him if he proposes to her.

"Are you saying that you are falling in love with somebody who has no time for you or who does not care about you?" I asked surprised.

"I think he likes me too." She replied.

"Think?" I asked "What makes you think that?"

"He always appears to want to tell me something" she said "but I suspect he has not been able to summon up the courage to do it."

"Well, that's great." I said "I did not know my innocent baby had grown old enough to sense things like that."

"It is quite obvious mum." she said. "Each time we meet, he always manages to get me to a corner."

"And then?" I asked

"It would appear all the courage he must have gathered for such an encounter simply slips out of him. He suddenly starts talking about my hair, my dress or my shoes."

"And not a word of love?" I asked.

"None mother." she replied. "It is so frustrating. When you like a guy you want him to say the word so that you accept and beam around with happiness. When he raises your hopes by taking you to a corner and does not end up landing, you feel really disappointed."

"Poor child." that was all I could say.

"My friend Nangel advised me to lead the bloke on and encourage him, but I can't do it." she continued. "How could I be leading a man to woo me? I would look cheap."

"That is true my child." I said.

"On the other hand Bichia my classmate advises me to rather play tough when eventually he proposes. She advises that I should put as many speed brakes as possible on his way and push him to do a lot of spade work before getting to his target. That way you earn a lot of respect from him."

"If you ask me," I found myself advising "your man has already shown a lot of shyness and timidity. Although I will not ask you to lead him on, I will caution you against any speed brakes. These speed brakes would discourage a prospective suitor and before you know it he would have turned in despair and proposed to that same friend who advised you to put speed brakes, and believe me, she will accept without any hesitation."

"Thank you mum for the advice." she said "I have been so confused. I suppose older men around your age have a different approach."

"True. When men get to forty and above they no longer beat around the bush or act shy when they want to get a woman. They simply joke into it and the woman suddenly realizes that she has been wrapped in."

"I suppose you met dad when you were about my age" she said.

"Older." I insisted.

"I would have loved to witness it." Titi said "How did you meet him? Was it love at first sight? Was there some feet dragging when dad was proposing, or he used the blunt approach of just saying 'hey, why don't we get married?'"

59

"You have asked too many questions at once." I protested. "Which one do you expect me to answer?"

"Just take one at a time mum" she answered. "If you forget anything, I will take you there."

"Love at first sight?" I asked "Well there are a few dashing men around for whom many women may think that they have fallen for at first sight, but that could be very misleading. Love is a sacred thing that is developed. It doesn't just come like a thunderbolt or cupid's arrow that strikes suddenly. There is much more in real love than simple appearance. Good looks count but it has to be spiced with concern, good behaviour or character, neatness, patience, understanding and other aspects. When you have these in a man, then you can truly fall in love with him. Otherwise, it is simple infatuation. I hope you are seeing all these in this Tangnankoli you believe you have fallen for."

"I have known him only for one month." She replied. "It should take years to identify all those qualities you have just named in a man."

"Even in a month, if you are careful and attentive, you could identify them. Hasty marriages based on simple infatuation don't last. That is why we have many cases of divorce in America and Europe. Would be couples don't take time to know each other well. A woman simply falls for a man because he is very handsome and shortly after, discovers that she has a monster for a husband."

"But if a woman should marry only a man that she truly loves, then many women will never get married because the right man may never come to propose." Titi said.

"Bravo", I said congratulating her. "You have reasoned like a woman. You have now seen that loving a man at first sight does not push him to equally love you and propose to you. As women, we are compelled to accept the best that comes and not necessarily the best that we would have liked. Until there is a change in this world where women are free to make their choice of a husband and propose to him the way men choose a wife and propose to her, only then can we reduce the incidence of divorce and have happier homes."

"You have just said it mama", Titi said. "I could have easily proposed to this feet dragging Tangnankoli and developed a happy home with him. Who knows, he may never be able to make up his mind and I might end up with some stupid jerk that is bold enough to propose."

"I believe it is still too early for you to start seriously thinking about marriage." I said carefully. "Why don't you concentrate on your studies for now? This is not the end of the world and many handsome young men will come proposing when the time is ripe."

"When will it be ripe enough for me to consider marriage?" Titi asked. "After Tangnankoli, I may never meet another man I really love."

"That is an illusion my dear daughter.", I said. "You are a beautiful and attractive girl and I am sure many valiant young men will come along, and it will be left for you to accept or reject. Some women are never proposed to and things become so desperate that they are prepared to accept any bloke who comes. These are women who could have been happily married if society would allow them to propose to a man of their choice."

"And mum", Titi added, "in one of the books we read in school, the author dwelt much on the tradition in some remote tribes where bride price is paid for a baby girl. She grows up with a husband already prepared for her."

"That is common in some parts of Africa", I said. "In Asia and other parts of the world, girls are forced into marriage at the age of twelve. Elsewhere girls are handed over to creditors so as to erase debts owed by their parents. In all these cases, the girl simply has no choice."

"There is a lot of unfairness against the female sex", Titi said.

"Much of this was embedded in tradition and societal norms", I said. "That is why you see that even in supposedly free countries like America and Britain where women are said to have every right, it is still the man that comes proposing for marriage."

"I suppose it is because women prefer it like that", said Titi.

"Maybe," I said "but I believe that someday things will change and women too will find it normal to propose to any man of their choice. In some areas of the Northwest region of Cameroon, women used to weep on their wedding day to give the impression that they were not very enthusiastic and too eager to marry a man and live their parents and siblings. But today things have changed and during weddings, you find the young brides rejoicing even more than the grooms."

"And polygamy is still very rife in Africa." Titi said "Why should men have the right to marry more than one wife?"

"Tradition and societal norms are still to be blamed." I said. "In some parts of the world it is normal and accepted for a husband to openly have concubines, whereas it is scandalous to hear that a wife has a lover."

"I am sure men do cheat on their wives because they are the ones that choose them and propose to them" Titi said.

"There, I would not know what to say." I admitted frankly.

"But mum," she asked "how can you know that your man is cheating?"

"It is not quite difficult dear," I said, "but one of the simplest ways to know is if he comes home late for no good reason and does not smell of alcohol. If not held back by work or some explainable reason, a man keeps late nights either if he is out drinking with friends or in bed with another woman."

Titi was silent for a while. I was happy that the worrisome conversation had come to an end when she suddenly said "I suppose it is the women who are to be blamed for all the negative forces directed at them. If you watch shows and public displays women are often scantily dressed, and virtually naked, whereas with the men it is different. Apart from those huge ugly wrestlers who dress in tight underpants. Most men are fully or even nattily dressed in public shows. Mama, why would women want to show off their bodies at the least opportunity?"

"It is a sign of feminism dear. The body of a young woman is quite smooth and beautiful while a man's body is hard and not very attractive to watch. You can equally see that when women grow older and become flabby, they no longer expose their bodies."

"And I have noticed," said Titi "that being feminine stretches to flirtatious attitudes. Mum, is it alright when women flirt with men? To me, it gives the impression to the man that the women are available, and the door could be open for him if he approached."

"Flirting is one of the traits of a woman," I said. "but it depends on how she does it. She could use it to attract a potential suitor, to take advantage of a man, to get a favour or simply to breakthrough into whatever she wants to achieve or get."

For the next two weeks all Titi's topics of conversation revolved only around Tangnankoli. His neat dressing, his attractive low cut hair, his smile, his voice, his intelligence and all the exaggerated good things about him were continuously ventilated by the love sick Titi as if there were no other topics in the world worth discussing. Tangnankoli did not seem to have any flaws or shortcomings but for the fact that he could not summon enough courage to propose to Titi.

"I am sure your friends are all fed up with your gross infatuation for this timid guy." I said one evening.

"Mum," she replied. "He is not timid. I am sure it is just that he wants to put it the right way. He's got feelings you know and lots of concern, and probably worries about how I would take any word that comes from his wonderful lips. He is not like those crude blokes who just go proposing carelessly without giving a girl the chance to hesitate and accept in a dignified manner."

I had my reservations but I held them back. The boy could be out right gay or maybe he was simply nursing a platonic love for her. It was equally possible that he was not even capable of making love. In my years on Earth, I have known a few friends who have fallen head over heels for a guy just to discover in the end that he was impotent, disappointingly undersexed or had a very diminutive penis. I thought I should let my daughter's exuberance for the affair die down before attempting to reason with her.

One week later I was out shopping with Titi when she pointed out a strikingly handsome woman to me.

"That is Tangnankoli's mother." she whispered.

"Have you ever met her?" I asked

"I have seen her only from a distance on a few occasions. Tangnankoli tells me she is very difficult and dictatorial. She even orders Tangnankoli's father around. Mum, I must admit that I am really scared of her."

Tangnankoli's mother actually looked forbidding with a very stern look on her face. She was also wearing an angry frown whereas nobody was provoking or challenging her.

I could not help smiling at Titi's statement about being scared.

"How would you cope with such a formidable lady as a mother-in-law?" I asked. "She might even decide to transfer and live with you and your husband if you eventually get married."

"Don't say that again mum." Titi said "That would be quite terrible. I don't think it is possible." She had lowered her head.

Titi suddenly raised her worried eyes towards me.

"Mum why did you say that about her insisting on living with us?" she asked "I think it is not normal that a woman leaves her husband and transfers to stay permanently with a different married couple even if her son is involved."

"Some women can do it." I insisted.

"That would be absurd." Titi said "Why would any right-thinking woman consider such a thing?"

"I don't know." I replied "But don't forget that many women are quite attached to their sons whom they always consider as their lovely little boys. Such women never trust any other female and always strive to protect the young man even though he is grown up and married."

"Tangnankoli's mother may look forbidding," Titi said "but she is not like that."

"That is a bit of wishful thinking." I said "After all you are dying to make her your mother-in-law."

I reflected for a while and thought I should use this opportunity to dissuade Titi from what I thought was a premature and early infatuation. Titi was barely twenty one and already thinking of leaving our home and living with a man permanently. It was something I was still not able to accept but these are modern days and you must tread carefully when handling a lovesick daughter.

"From the way your love bird's mother looks," I continued "she is most certainly one of those females who would want to keep a strict eye on the way their son is treated by his wife. She would want to control what you cook and serve him to eat, control the company both of you keep and the meeting groups you are engaged with, decide who should come to your house, the number of children you should have and the names they should be given. Don't be surprised if all your lovely children end up with scandalously odd biblical names just because your mother-in-law wishes to appease some ancient relatives of hers."

"Oh stop it mum." Titi said "You are making my flesh to creep. Anyway, I love Tangnankoli so much that I am certain we would make a happy home despite any interference from a misguided mother-in-law. I will cope with her just to be with my sweet heart."

Titi was silent for a while. I could see that despite the brave statement, she was worried. Finally, she looked at me.

"Mum, would you have been that way if I were a boy?" she asked.

"Certainly not." I replied "Mothers come differently. Don't forget that you have two elder brothers who may want to get married someday. I intend to completely embrace their spouses and avoid in every way to interfere in their homes."

"I wish all mothers could be like you." She said

My daughter really looked worried.

"Do you know her name?" I asked looking in the direction of Tangnankoli's mother.

"She is Mrs. Timti." Titi replied

"Okay." I said "I will accost her and pick her brains a little. I hope it is all right with you."

"It is okay mother," Titi replied "but please do be tactful and careful."

"Trust me." I said to Titi. "I just want to find out if your future mother- in-law is malleable. She might have this stern external appearance but inside, she may have a heart of gold."

I wanted Titi to feel completely at ease.

Leaving Titi to do some eye shopping, I moved over to where Mrs. Timti was admiring a very outdated male suit. It looked expensive but I suppose no young man today would have thought of wearing it, even to please a concerned parent.

"Hello Mrs. Timti" I said smiling

"Do I know you?" she said with a rude frown.

"Not really." I replied smiling "But from the fact that I know your name, it means I know who you are. Ooh, what a nice suit you are admiring there."

I watched her closely. Her reaction was still stiff.

"Everybody respects you," I continued "so I could not pass you by without at least offering my humble greetings."

She relaxed a bit and examined me closely. She saw in front of her a shapely lady, well dressed, wearing an expensive perfume and certainly of class. She decided that she could talk to me.

"I can see you like this beautiful suit." she said. "It means you at least have some taste."

"It would be wonderful on your man I am sure." I said encouragingly. Who would she be buying that kind of suit for if not her husband who would certainly be on the leeward side of life?

"You have eyes too." she said "I want to give my little boy a surprise. His birthday is around the corner and I want him to wear this nice suit on that day."

"How wonderful." I said doubtfully.

"You can't trust these little darlings when it comes to buying clothes that are good for them." she continued "If you allow them to buy these things, they surface with funny items. They always need close guidance."

"So, you are shopping for his birthday?" I asked

"Yes," she replied "I wish to give him a birthday party. Look at the shoes I have chosen for him to wear along with this nice suit that I have just discovered. He wears size forty three."

She showed a pair of expensive but very ugly shoes in a shopping basket she was carrying.

"I don't like those tight small things these children like to wear these days." She said. "A man's feet should be free and relaxed."

I eyed the shoes with distaste but smiled all the same.

"How lucky the young man is." I said "Not all young men have concerned mothers like you."

"Thank you." she said actually smiling for her first time. "And when you fix them up like this, some hopeless girl comes lurking around and before you know what is happening your son is hooked up to some jezebel."

"Do you think all girls are bad?" I asked. "Your son needs to have a few dates and eventually get married. I also have a daughter and I understand if she has a young man for a date."

"That would be a misguided thing to do." She replied harshly "I don't even want to hear that word dating, let alone the word marriage."

"But you got married" I pointed out. "You are Mrs. Timti and you had your son through marriage."

"May be," she acknowledged "but in our days we were quite good and could make good wives. Today all girls are rotten, exposed to pornography, wild life, hard drugs, careless promiscuity and emancipation. I would not want any wretched female to go cheating on my innocent little boy and even attempt to override him because some blasted feminist said so."

"Are you saying that your son has no female friends that you know of?" I asked incredulously

"If I found out that he had one," she said sternly "I would kill her. What can a young bitch do to my son apart from leading him into the gutter? I won't allow my little boy to end up a failure in life."

"That is an extreme thing to say." I replied.

"I don't mince words." she said "I mean what I am saying and my son knows it. I give him whatever he wants and control him completely. The day I will see a wonderfully good girl of my choice, I will then give him a wife."

I was wondering how Titi would take that kind of information. Titi was a young sensitive girl and I am sure, would constantly be hurt if she ended up as Mrs. Timti's daughter in law. I was however comforted by the fact that Tangnongkoli might likely never summon enough courage to

69

propose. Even if he did, his mother would certainly not accept any woman that was brought by the son.

Back at home I sat down with Titi

"That woman is really tough." I said

"Marriage is for better or for worse." Titi said "I will have to take it like that."

"Titi you are sounding as if you are already married to Tangnongkoli. He has not yet proposed to you and you don't even know whether his mother will accept you."

"These are modern days." said Titi "Mothers should not be the ones to choose wives for their sons."

"That may be how it should be," I said "but from my conversation with that woman she is quite determined to be the one to choose a wife for her son."

"Tangnongkoli will not accept that." Titi said with emphasis "I am sure he loves me."

"You think so?" I asked. "The young man may be hesitating to propose to you simply because he is scared of what his mother will say. He has already proven that he lacks courage and with a mother like that breathing over his neck, I wonder whether he will be able to have a say in his marriage."

Titi went to the refrigerator for some fruit juice.

"Will you have some?" she asked.

"Yes." I replied. "Thank you."

Titi brought me a glass and poured fruit juice from a pitcher.

"Titi? How do you intend to get this timid guy to propose to you?" I asked.

"Mum, he has invited me to his birthday party." she said "I am quite sure that this time he will say the word."

"Does he live in his own place?" I asked

"He lives with his parents." Titi said "His mother will not allow him to move out to a place of his own."

"You see what I was telling you?" I asked. "He is just a mama's boy.

"Mum, let's leave it till the birthday party tomorrow." She said "If I come back from there without him proposing, then I will simply have to forget about him."

"At what time is the party?" I asked.

"It starts at 12 noon." Titi said.

"Is that not a bit early?" I asked.

"His mother insisted that it should start early so that everybody leaves her house early. The party will last till 5 o'clock."

"I would like to see what kind of party it will be." I said. "With that strict woman in charge, it may turn out to be as dull as a prayer session in one of those old traditional churches."

I was sure the birthday party was certainly going to be far from lively.

The next day, Titi left for the party at a few minutes to twelve. I had no particular place to go to on that day and Akoni had gone out with some friends. I tried to occupy myself in one way or another, hoping that Titi was having a swell time at the party. I was therefore surprised when Titi came back home from the party at 4 pm, looking quite frustrated.

"You don't look like a young woman who has just been revelling." I said.

"It was catastrophic mum." Titi said.

"Was the food that bad? Were there no drinks?" I asked.

"There was much mum." She said. "There were all the nice things to eat although there was no alcohol."

"You don't take alcohol," I said, "so you certainly had no problem."

"But the old witch would not allow us to feel free." Titi said. "She sat there almost throughout, closely monitoring her son and everything that was going on."

"So you had to bear her unwanted presence almost throughout the party?" I asked.

"Yes." Titi said "She went out briefly only at one point. I suppose she went to ease herself."

"You are back rather early." I said. "The party must really have been boring. Did Tangnankoli end up proposing?"

"With his mother's presence, he developed cold feet." She said.

"Just what I had expected." I said. "That sissy is not really what is good for you."

"However," Titi said "the moment his mother went out, Tangnangkoli hastily led me out to the veranda."

"To propose I suppose." I said

"That is what I thought." Titi said. "My heart was beating with anticipation."

"So did he manage to say it?" I asked "Did he go down on his knees, and beg you to be his bride and make his world happy?"

"That is the problem mum." Titi said "We were rudely interrupted by his mother who suddenly appeared on the veranda."

"I thought you said she had gone to the toilet or somewhere." I said "Where did she suddenly surface from?"

"I suppose she had come back from wherever she had gone to and missed her little boy immediately." Titi said.

"I am sure there was much unpleasantness at that point." I said.

"You should have seen the way she shouted at us and ordered me out of her house before I spoiled her little boy." Titi said "Mum, she called me terrible names."

"And Tangnagkoli did not fly to the rescue of the woman he loves?" I asked.

"You were right mum." Titi said "The bloke is simply a mama's boy. Instead of defending me, he rather concentrated on pleading with his mum to forgive him. He did not even bother to see me off.'

"Love is dead I suppose?" I said

"Completely dead, mum." Titi replied

I heaved a sigh of relief. Titi was too young to fall head long in love and Tangnakoli was not the right person for her.

5

Mawumi

I was fast asleep when suddenly the door of the bedroom made a slight noise. I may be a sound sleeper but at times the slightest noise gets me out of even the deepest sleep. I opened my eyes in the dark and listened carefully. Someone was trying to close the door as carefully as possible so that there should be no noise from the action. Then, assuming that he had succeeded in slipping into the room without waking me up, the furtive person started tip toeing to the bed. Just then I reached out for the bedside switch and put on the lights. Although I would not have expected anybody else apart from my husband to be entering my room at that time of the night, I was kind of surprised at what I saw.

Akoni was standing half way to the bed looking very embarrassed and ashamed. He had come back home late a few times before but each time he had had a plausible reason and always informed me earlier that he would come home a bit late. Right now, he knew he was as guilty as sin and had probably not had time to cook up a convincing excuse before coming home. Besides, he was stinking of alcohol and the stench filled the whole room, virtually choking me. I stared at him without knowing what to say.

"I am sorry dear", he said guiltily before I could say anything.

I must admit, I was a bit confused. I did not know whether to feel sorry for him or to pounce on him like a tigress. I simply frowned and kept quiet. This hurt him much more than if I had shouted back.

"You are not mad at me, I hope." he finally said after a brief interval.

I kept staring at him in silence. He shifted from one leg to the other.

"Say something dear, I have told you I am sorry." He said "It is Ndichia who invited me for a drink after work and things became hectic. He kept urging me to drink and telling me that for once I should act like a man."

I was tempted to ask him if he had been acting like a woman since we got married but overcame this temptation and let it go. I really did not know whether to feel sorry for Akoni or flare up.

"He was of the opinion that a man had to show that he had control in his home and over his wife, and the best way to do it was to go home late and soused once in a while." Akoni continued stupidly.

I still struggled to restrain myself from uttering a word. Akoni had certainly gone way beyond his limit with the booze otherwise he would not have been repeating such stupidities. But my silence was pushing him on to reveal things. Akoni was no squealer and under normal circumstances would not have been revealing to me what Ndichia had been saying, possibly under the influence of alcohol too. However, *in vino veritas* our Roman forefathers used to say when thinking of the club of Bacchus the Roman God of wine.

"He said," continued Akoni "that all this while I had adopted the wrong precedence and that a man needed to make his wife get used to the fact that he could come home late whenever he wanted."

I still said nothing.

"Ndichia pointed out that his own wife was always rather surprised when at times he got home early."

I could no longer keep quiet. It was too much. It would have been better for Akoni to just keep quiet rather than ranting like that.

"Why don't you go back to him then?" I asked "Go and spend the rest of the night with Ndichia and leave me in peace."

I could have congratulated myself for the calm I had exhibited but was disturbed by this new turn in Akoni's life.

He had mentioned that he had been out boozing with Ndichia and that was just the problem. Ndichia was one of those gooks who believed that before you retire each day, you must have gallons of some alcoholic brew sloshing inside you. He was known for late nights and loose behaviour. He was very popular with bar girls and prostitutes and they in turn felt very free with him. Because of all these shortcomings his wife, a quiet self-respecting woman would not be seen in public places with him. Of course he took advantage of this and exaggerated his frivolous lifestyle.

Ndichia was equally not the type of person you would want to have your husband hobnobbing with. Apart from the booze he could lure honest husbands into seeing other women. His scandalous relationship with women who had no respect for themselves made him to consider all women as very low creatures that are always willing to jump into bed with a man, for sex or for money.

"Akoni," I said calmly "I am not ready to fight with you now. I simply want you to be reasonable. Ndichia is not the kind of person you should get close to or have as a friend. You have many good friends, Chiambeng, Kimeng, Kimbi, you name them. What do you want to do with a rustic like Ndichia?"

Akoni remained standing where he was, looking stupidly at me. He must have had several litres more than his system could contain. The womanly spirit in me however finally overcame everything.

"Don't keep standing there like a statue." I said. "Remove those stinking clothes and get into bed."

He obliged immediately. I could see that he was really sorry for what he had done that night. It was not long before he fell into sleep and started snoring like a witch's cauldron bubbling over with some strange concoction.

The next day I avoided bringing up the topic as I saw a lot of remorse all over Akoni's face. When I told my friend Nakoma during the day she laughed and told me to be careful about any friendship ties between Akoni and that scoundrel Ndichia. She told me her husband came home soused once in a while but she was always comfortable with the fact that he was not out drowning himself in Ndichia's company. She said her only problem was that her husband snored whenever he came home drunk and that the snoring could be likened to one of these kettles that whistle to indicate that the water inside is boiling.

For two weeks Akoni was exemplary. He was really the model of a good husband and I was really proud of him. Then, one fateful day I went to his office to discuss something. As his wife, the secretary never stopped me from entering for they had been made to understand that Akoni never kept secrets from me. As I strolled confidently into the office, I could have been knocked off my feet by the scene I saw. Akoni was entertaining Ndichia and some blasted girl to whiskey and Martini which he kept in a cupboard in the office. To make it worse he had also offered them snacks that I had personally taken the effort to keep in his office for important guests. As I moved into the office struggling to control my anger, the sexily dressed jezebel hungrily filled her mouth with doughnuts and chased it down with a large greedy gulp of martini on the rocks, as if she wanted to finish the bottle before somebody else came to share it.

"Welcome madam," said Ndichia smiling broadly as if we were best of friends. "I just dropped by with Miss Visi to brighten up your husband's, life a little. They say all work and no play makes Jack a dull boy and they are right. Your husband should learn to relax and have fun, not live a dull life of work to home and from home to work."

If I were one of those temperamental females, I would have broken a bottle on the arrogant bloke's head. I rather took a deep breath and concentrated on my husband.

"I was not expecting you dear." Akoni said before realizing that he had said just the wrong thing.

"I can see that you are enjoying yourself thoroughly" I said sarcastically. "How would you expect me?"

Akoni rushed to make introductions which I suspected was an attempt to prevent Visi from saying something stupid.

"Visi, this is my wife Mawumi." He said patting my arm clumsily. He had stood up to receive me and possibly prove that he had nothing to do with Visi.

"This is Ndichia's friend, Visi." He said, "Please do sit down."

The atmosphere was choking.

"I did not mean to stay long." I said trying to be as calm as possible. "I just stopped by because I happened to have been around your office. Well, see you at home."

I went out of the office and left them to whatever fun they were having. But all along the way and back in my office I could not think of anything else but the scene I had just witnessed in Akoni's office. Ndichia was bad company and there he was sitting in Akoni's office and feeling free. To make matters worse, he had brought along an attractive female, a bit on the flamboyant side but full of curves and seduction. She looked much more like one of those rapacious birds, ready to pounce on Akoni if given the least chance. I couldn't quite say whether she was one of Ndichia's numerous girlfriends or Ndichia had brought her as a tempting piece of bait to lure Akoni into becoming 'a real man' as he would have put it. To the distorted reasoning of Ndichia, a real man was one who over indulged in alcohol, always came home late and never gave a damn to what his wife said, and most of all, sampled other females without restraint as long as they were willing.

My head was ticking and my pressure was up. I could not stop suspecting that Akoni was up to something with Ndichia and the girl. Of course only a stupid man would easily admit to his wife that he was cheating on her, so I needed to plan my line of questioning well in other to establish the real position of things. I really needed to know whether I was worrying myself sick for no reason or there was actually something to worry about. Some women have been known to attempt suicide simply because they were convinced that their man was cheating on them, only to find out that there was actually nothing but some gross misunderstanding.

That evening, I received my husband back home as if nothing had happened. While we were in the living room enjoying a soap opera with Titi and one of my sons who had come visiting, I laughed along and commented on certain actions in the film without giving the least hint that there was something amiss. It was when we had retired to the room and locked the door that I confronted Akoni.

"So, Ndichia has been frequenting your office?" I asked. "You seem to have become close friends."

"Not really" Akoni replied. "He has been trying to impose himself on me but I have done my best to avoid him. I have been shunning all his invitations to go out for drinks so he came to my office."

"And brought along a woman to show you what you have been missing or was she a special gift?" I asked angrily "Looking at the reception party I met in your office, Ndichia seemed like a regular visitor and somebody you entertain often."

"Women! Women!" Akoni said exasperated. "He came to my office with a visitor so I had at least to do some entertaining."

"Visitor?" I said "Whose visitor was it? Anyway, for how long have you known that girl?"

I suddenly realized that my tone was going up. I had to calm down a little.

"I saw her yesterday for my first time." Akoni said "She is Ndichia's friend for Christ sake."

"She did not seem like a stranger in that office." I said "She was well ensconced as if she was a partner to the business."

"Mawumi!" Akoni said "Watch what you are saying."

"Anyway," I said "you are aware of the fact that Ndichia is married. Why were you tolerating him and his girlfriend? Is that what you men do when your wives are not around?"

Akoni was somehow trapped but struggled to slip out of the knot.

"Ndichia came to my office with a friend. A friend must not necessarily be a man, and a female friend must not be a lover. We have platonic female friends you know."

"You call that hawk a platonic female friend?" I asked

"Whatever she is," Akoni said, "I did not have to go into that."

"Maybe because Ndichia brought her to hand over to you?" I said in anger. "I could see the way she was ogling at you with lots of lust."

"There," said Akoni heatedly "you are going too far."

I could not hold myself again. I burst into tears.

"Calm down." Akoni said smoothening my hair. "Please calm down and be reasonable. Okay I will never allow Ndichia into my presence again. I will tell him clearly that I prefer to keep my family intact than to be seen with him anywhere."

"You would?" I said between sobs

"I mean what I say." Akoni said reassuringly. "Just keep quiet and be a good girl. I can't do anything in this world to hurt you and you know it. Now look at my face and smile."

I was completely disarmed.

There was much bliss for the next two months and Akoni was as loving and caring as ever. He came home late once in a while but each time he brought something nice to keep me from grumbling. Apart from that, he bought me nice presents more frequently. I was really wallowing in happiness, completely oblivious of the implications of the saying, 'Beware of the Greeks, especially when they come bearing gifts.' The Trojans had tasted this wise saying before and knew better. I was soon to understand it well too. Akoni was in no way a Greek but what he did to me was just like what the Greeks had done to the Trojans.

It all started when I noticed Akoni making a furtive call. There was network all over but he went out to the veranda and talked in hushed tones. Shortly after, he gave some excuse and went out. Two days later his phone rang as we sat discussing the possibilities of sending our daughter to Europe for studies. Instead of answering the phone right where he was sitting, as usual, he jumped up and rushed out to the veranda. It was then that something pricked me as odd and I started closely monitoring his reactions to his calls. It did not take me long to realize that there were certain calls that were not meant for my ears. Either he made or received such calls in the toilet or out on the veranda where he could not be overheard.

I was no sleuth but I decided to play the fool and dig into the whole thing. There were several possibilities either he was now keeping bad company or seeing some other woman, or women? But then, he could rather be in trouble. It was possible that he was being blackmailed. But who would want to blackmail him, and based on what secret sordid information that could ruin him?

"It was Ndichia's wife who finally tipped me about the situation. I was surprised to find her waiting in my office one afternoon when I went back from lunch. She was looking calm as usual and did not have the appearance of a woman, carrying explosive information. Her husband's wayward attitudes had compelled her to develop a heart of stone.

"I am happy you did not have to take too long" she said as I came in

"Welcome Nindum." I said.

We were not close friends but knew each other.

"You are certainly surprised to see me here." She said.

"I cannot pretend about that." I replied. "You have never been to see me before."

"Well," she said. "Circumstances have forced me this time to. I hope you are not too busy."

"Feel free." I said.

"We really need to talk." She said and moved her chair closer.

"Talk?" I asked. "About whom?"

"About our husbands." she replied

"What about them?" I asked feigning nonchalance.

"My husband seems to have dragged yours into his dirty lifestyle." she said "I thought you should know. Please forgive me if I am doing the wrong thing."

"No" I said. "You are doing the right thing. You came to me like a fellow woman to brief me on a situation that involves me and my happiness. Thank you."

"I am glad to hear that." she replied.

"Now tell me," I said. "Into what mess has your husband actually placed mine?"

"They often drink together, only that your husband strives to leave for home earlier. My husband seems to have transformed your husband into his drinking mate by providing him with some stuff that prevents a man from getting drunk and considerably takes off the smell of the alcohol."

"Strange." I said calmly.

My husband actually smelt of something strange when he came home at times but in my happy mood, I had never bothered.

"That is not all." said Ndichia's wife. "What really ties the two together is that they have these twins as girlfriends."

"What?" I shouted.

"Yes." She replied. "One of them is called Visi, I suppose and your husband has been saddled with the twin sister or vice versa."

"Are you sure of what you are saying?" I asked quite hurt and almost on the verge of tears.

Ndichia's wife was quite used to her husband's numerous escapades and did not seem to worry much. She was quite calm.

"Don't take it too badly." she said. "Men are like that. You simply have to be happy that after everything he comes back home to you. Always receive him well otherwise you will drive him back into the ever waiting arms of those free women."

I was staring at the wall opposite me seeing nothing. My eyes were glistening with unshed tears.

How could Akoni do such a thing? He had promised never to go hobnobbing with the perfidious Ndichia and here were they sharing the same adulterous relationships. What a fool I had been all along.

After Ndichia's wife left, I continued to sit and stare. Just then an elderly colleague came in. She had been married for close to thirty years and seemed to be satisfied with it. It was not difficult for her to discern that there was something wrong.

"I just discovered that my husband is cheating on me." I said in response to her questioning look.

"Mr. Akoni Ngongnuwi?" she said in disbelief.

Within our circles Akoni was known to be an exemplary husband.

"You cannot take this lying down." She advised "Fight back or you may lose your husband to some half-baked female. Akoni is too good and handsome for you to let go like that."

"How do I fight?" I said helplessly "I don't even know with whom he is cheating."

"Find out where this woman is and warn her to leave your husband alone." My colleague said "Threaten her with witchcraft and bundles of ill luck."

"Some of these women could become very provocative. They always have wagging tongues ready to strike back." I said

"Then increase the torrent of abuses on her." My colleague insisted "You can even adopt physical violence as a means to scare her completely out of her wits. Take some of us along and we shall back you up."

"I don't intend to go into a fight because of a man who has no respect for himself." I said "Besides, some of these street women are real fighters and have nothing to lose."

"Anyway," the colleague said. "To guarantee a proper ending to the whole thing you must also turn on your husband at home and use your tongue to lash him to no extent. Even if the bitch of a girl wants to continue luring your husband to her bed you would have scared him from making any further attempts."

"I will think about it." I said in an attempt to dismiss her.

Some women can provoke a conflagration from a few sparks. It is quite debasing to go attacking woman openly on the suspicion that they are sleeping with your husband. If he did not go after them or accept them, nothing like that would have happened.

I called my elder sister and told her about my distress.

"You should pack and come to me or go home to mum." she advised as soon as I had told her the whole story. The dog does not deserve you."

"That I should leave my home and husband and transfer elsewhere?" I asked.

"Women do it every day" my sister said. "Because of cheating or battery, women abandon their homes until when the man begs and sincerely proves that he has changed."

I considered this option and thought it was not right. The home was mine. I developed it alongside with my husband and had come to feel very comfortable in it. Everything was placed where I wanted it to be and I did not need anybody's permission to do whatever I wanted.

Then, I thought of the last option. The first thing was to let my husband know that I was aware of his shameful relationship. The next thing was to pack out of our bedroom and move into another one. Finally, there would be no speech between us. If truly he felt something for me, he could be quite hurt and lonely and seek to reform. If on the other hand the flame I awakened in Akoni had died and he was now totally enamoured by his new found love, then I would make his stay in that house lonely and miserable and he may end up packing out instead to join his new catch.

I was thus determined to calmly tell him that I was fully aware of his love affair and stop there. No scolding, no shouting, no questioning and no pleading, just total silence and aloofness.

After letting Akoni know that I was aware of his relationship with the twins, I transferred to one of our spare rooms next to Titi's. My two boys who might have ended up sympathizing with their father were all away and my daughter was fully behind me. It was quite tedious for her but somehow she managed to completely ignore and snub the father she loved very much. We made sure Akoni's food was served on the table and left him to eat alone. I had completely abandoned the bedroom to him and did not care whether he kept it tidy or not.

The first two days of this treatment were not quite successful however, and Titi and I were scared that we might have taken the wrong approach. After the total boycott of the first day, Akoni came home the next two nights quite drunk. He did not bother about the food we had kept for him and simply slipped into his bedroom. It was not certain whether he had been out drinking alone or with Ndichia, or possibly with the girl friends.

After two days of such behaviour however; he seemed to have come back to his senses. He came home early and directly from work each day, ate his food like a good husband, sat watching television for a while and retired to his room to sleep. To avoid any contacts with him, Titi and I went off to our bedrooms each time we heard him drive in.

On a few occasions we came face to face in the house but no words were exchanged. However each time, I could see the strain on his face.

At the end of one week desperation obliged him to act. I heard a knock on my door after he had come home that evening and had his meal. I neither answered nor invited him in but he opened the door and came in all the same.

"Mawumi," he said "I can no longer stand this. We cannot continue living like this."

"I thought we were not on talking terms." I reminded him. "Go back to your street women if you need to talk to somebody."

I concentrated on the book I was reading and gave no heed to what he was trying to say. The poet who declared that 'Hell hath no fury like a woman scorned' should have adjusted it to 'Hell hath no fury like a women deceived.'

Akoni finally discovered that he was making no headway and that it was not going to be easy to soften the heart of a woman who was proving more stubborn than a mule, and slipped off to his room.

The next day he adopted a different approach. Instead of coming to my room, he made a bee line for Titi's room after his evening meal. His efforts to tip toe to the room did not prevent me from guessing what was happening. What transpired in the room? I could not know. It would have been quite awkward for me to go eavesdropping too.

The next day Titi came back from school bringing along her friend Sih.

"Mum, it is good you are home" she said.

"Why?" I asked "Did somebody send you to me?"

I remembered that Akoni had had been in her room the previous night,

"Kind of" she said "but I don't really know how to put it."

"Is that why you brought your friend along?" I asked wondering why she would want to discuss something delicate like that in the presence of outsiders.

"I am sorry to be intruding into what looks like a family crises auntie." Sih said "But Titi insisted that I come, and I also thought that it was necessary for me to."

I frowned and waited for her to continue, after all she seemed to have been informed about the whole situation.

"Auntie," she continued. "My friend's life has been quite miserable all these past days. She is no longer attentive in class and has become quite passive. She remains sad and dull and shies away from everybody. Titi is very worried and whatever is worrying her must be cleared off before it ruins her life. A young girl needs to be sprite and happy."

I discovered that in my blind fury and determination to punish Akoni is no uncertain manner, I had completely forgotten to consider the feelings of my daughter. Daughters are generally very attached to their fathers and to treat them with aloofness takes a great effort. Besides, an extended quarrel between a husband and wife always takes its toll on the children.

"Thank you very much." I told Sih "I will consider what you have just said very seriously."

I waited for Sih to leave and then turned to Titi.

"What did your father tell you yesterday night?" I asked.

"You noticed that he came to my room in the night?" she asked.

"I heard furtive footsteps" I said. "What did you people discuss?"

"Mum, "she said "You needed to see daddy yesterday night when he came to talk to me. His eyes were glistening with tears. I am sure he made a terrible effort not to burst into tears."

I was silent.

"Mum." Titi continued "Daddy is really sorry for what he did. I think you should really rethink this stand of yours.

I was making a terrible effort to concentrate.

"Daddy told me about the effort he made to summon enough courage to approach you and how you rebuffed his effort without opening even a small window. He has been through hell all these days and his biggest wish in this world is to hold you in his arms."

Titi was quiet for a while. I could see she was trying to hold back tears.

"Mummy," she finally said "coming home from school used to be like going back to a paradise. That was when we were all happy, shared our meals together and ate with much appetite, and watched TV happily together before you people retired to your room. We always got up in the morning and started the day like one happy family. Now, coming back from school is like going to a hell house where there is nothing but groaning and gnashing of teeth."

I was really overwhelmed. It had not been easy for me either. You can't punish a man you love, the way I was trying to punish Akoni, without punishing yourself too. I missed him in bed, and missed his interesting company and conversation. But now, I realized that I had inadvertently punished my daughter along with my husband. I was determined to give in, but in a dignified way.

"I am sorry Titi", I said at last "I did not realize how terribly all this has been affecting you. I am truly sorry."

I patted her jaw lovingly.

"Now smile and consider this as all over." I cooed to her "We shall not fight again. Your father has realized what he did wrong and how hurtful it can be. I for my part have realized that attempting to punish a man blindly may take its toll on innocent children."

Titi shook her head and attempted to smile.

"And you Titi," I said, "you are a young woman who will certainly get married and have children someday. Always remember this incident and always remember that when two elephants fight the grass suffers. Your children should never find themselves in such a situation."

6

Matimi

It was break time and I was famished. It was one of those days when you get so involved with work that you don't realize the time is passing fast until your stomach tells you. I looked at my watch. It was a few minutes past one and my system needed refuelling. My husband Akoni had asked me to meet him at Chvu bar for lunch and I intended to be there on time. Each moment I spent with him was quite wonderful. As I came out of the office and moved towards the car, I remembered that Akoni always told me how he could enjoy even the worst food on Earth if he were eating in my company.

I drove off to Chvu bar and parked carefully. As I strode in, I was disappointed to see him sitting with a squat ugly fellow who looked like a cross between a bulldog and a bullfrog. It was Batifuomu the lawyer. Batifuomu was a bloke who had a very high opinion about himself. He was married to two wives and always boasted that no female could resist his advances. He was one of those chaps a woman would not want to sit close to as he would keep leaning against her, constantly placing his repulsive paws on her thighs as he boasted about his irresistible charms. Simply sitting with him on the same table was equally bad. His conversation was quite bawdy and left much to be desired. The worst was his eating habits. He chewed his food like a pig and was very wanting in table manners. However, there he was sitting with my husband on the same table and abusively drinking good wine, certainly bought by Akoni.

"I did not know you had company." I said giving my husband a peck on the jaw.

"What of this other juicy jaw over here?" Batifuomu said pointing at his left jaw.

"I can see it is really juicy" I said sarcastically eying his nasty jowls with disdain. "However, I will leave that for your two wives to sample."

"You women never know what is good for you." he grumbled. "Anyway sit down and have some good food and good vine with us."

"Are you paying?" I asked noticing the understanding smile on my husband's face.

Apart from the loathsome appearance and foul speech, Batifuomu further had the bad habit of always scrounging on others. If you saw him having a drink with any person it was certain that he was being offered that drink.

"What does it matter who is paying"? He said angrily "Akoni is my bosom friend. If he pays it is the same as me paying."

"He may be your friend," I said "but he is my husband. If he pays it is the same like the money is coming out of my purse."

"Sit down dear." Akoni said gently. "You came here to enjoy your lunch, so sit down and enjoy it."

I pulled the chair, closer to my husband and away from Batifuomu, and sat down wondering how I would enjoy my meal in the presence of such a nasty eater. Batifuomu was completely oblivious of his repulsive eating habits. The fact that he was as attractive as a hippo, and went on champing away at his food and slurping his wine as if he was drinking through a snorkel, did not help either, and made everything about him quite repulsive.

Akoni hailed the waiter who immediately made a bee line for our table. I ordered for a simple cheese sandwich and a Coke. I could not imagine myself enjoying cooked food in the presence of Batifuomu.

"I need to rush back to work and ordering a full dish will take some time," I explained to Akoni as I noticed the questioning look on his face, provoked by my request for a sandwich.

"If you say so." he said and concentrated on his own food.

He was having a steak although he often preferred African dishes. I was convinced that this choice was determined by the fact that he had to eat alongside a sloppy eater. Batifuomu had made a choice of cassava fufu and okra soup. For such a messy eater the combination was bad enough. To watch him eat while you were also having a meal was possible only if you had a stiff drink in front of you.

He cut off a huge chunk of fufu with huge fingers that looked like sausages rolled the chunk with his fingers into a ball, dipped the ball into the okra and virtually snapped at it as he sent it into his large gaping mouth. This exercise was repeated over and over, while in between, he slurped at the slimy okra with a lot of appetite.

Instead of concentrating on his meal, he turned and pointed at me with a huge messy finger. He was enjoying his food like a true African using his fingers rather than a fork and a knife. Okra was dribbling out of the corner of his mouth.

"What do you want to work for?" He asked. "Does your husband not give you enough money?"

"He gives me much more than you give your wives." I replied "I also give him when he needs and when I feel like."

The bloke turned to Akoni and frowned.

"You stoop that low to receiving money from a woman?" he asked "how do you know the money is not coming from a lover of hers?"

"She just mentioned that she is going back to work from here." Akoni said "She has a salary."

"That does not mean a thing." Batifuomu said "Women should stay at home, cook for us, wash our things, keep us comfortable in bed and make children for us. Women are very vulnerable my friend and allowing her to work for some company or for somebody means exposing her to temptation. There are many smart nattily dressed guys around with sharp tongues and these are lechers like me who are always prepared to sample other people's things. At the job side there are colleagues that do not know their limits and would seize any opportunity to pat your woman on the buttocks. The most dangerous out of this lot are bosses."

Akoni burst into laughter.

"You seem to have a very poor opinion about our women folk," he said to Batifuomu "Why did you get married then, and to two wives at that?"

"A man must get married somehow," replied Batifuomu, "but he needs to protect the women from wolves."

"Wolves are everywhere my friend." Akoni said. "If your wife does not work and stays home she is still exposed to neighbours and other persons that pass by."

"That is why I have two wives." said Batifuomu. "If one of them tries it, the other will certainly report her to me."

"Staying at home doesn't keep them fully busy." I said "At one time they become like idle prisoners who need fun and it is easier for them to stray off than for a working woman. You see, a working woman must be present at work otherwise she faces sanctions."

"They keep each other company so they cannot complain about boredom. There is always work in the house too so they can't complain of being idle." he said "Another reason why I married two of them is that as women, they will keep vying for my attention. They watch one another closely and that makes me comfortable."

"Could you imagine the day they may decide to cooperate with each other to enjoy themselves fully with other men?" Akoni asked

"God forbid bad things." Batifuomu said "That can never happen."

After my dry snack, I stood up to go.

"We are not yet tired of your company" Batifuomu said "It is always good to have a beautiful woman around you when you are relaxing."

"I am sorry." I said "but I need to go back to work."

"You see the trouble of having a working woman?" Batifuomu said to Akoni "You cannot control her any longer. Get back to work indeed. If you were my wife I would have horse whipped some sense into you."

"Fortunately for me, I could never have agreed to marry you for all the gold on earth." I said. "I can even have the pleasure of telling you that you turn me off completely. I wonder how your wives stand you."

He roared like a cuckolded lion and attempted to jump up and come at me but was restrained by my husband. He was actually boiling with rage, proof that he was certainly a wife beater.

Without even bothering to say good bye to my husband, I moved gracefully towards the door and took off.

That evening I came home sulking. I was determined to compel Akoni to choose the right type of friends and jettison trash like Batifuomu. After attempting to speak to me a few times and getting no reply, Akoni realised that he had some pleading and explaining to do and launched into it at once. I love my husband dearly and enjoy every minute we spend together. Every minute of discord between the two of us is therefore like a month in hell. I was thus prepared to listen to him and forget. After all he was so different from Batifuomu and some of the unbearable and over assuming males in town.

"That chap Batifuomu is incorrigible." Akoni said "I am sorry dear for all what transpired at Chvu bar.

"But why did you go inviting such a punk for lunch?" I asked angrily.

"I did not invite him." Akoni said "I am fully aware of the fact that he is not the kind of person to have a meal with and that his eating habits are appalling. You know very well that I barely tolerate his presence."

"How did he come to be sitting with you then?" I asked still feigning anger.

"He met me there and simply imposed himself on me."

"With such an odious person for company, why did you still ask me out for lunch?" This time I was no longer severe.

"He came and settled down after I had already called you." Akoni said. "I saw no reason for stopping you then. Besides, I so much wanted to have lunch with my dear wife."

The little anger in me dissipated completely at this last piece of flattery. Tell me a woman who does not enjoy being flattered, especially by a loving husband.

"I don't like that clumsy fellow at all." I said. "Everything about him is repulsive. If I were a judge, he would never win any case in my court."

Having straightened my husband on the issue, I bustled around to make him something nice to eat.

A week after the incident with Batifuomu, I was surprised when his first wife, Matimi visited my job site. She looked like she had been in a brawl with a tigress over a tiger. I was not too surprised, given my assessment of Batifuomu as a practicing wife beater. She had certainly been subject to battery from her hideous consort.

"Welcome my dear," I said "Sit down."

There was an elaborate sign hung in a conspicuous corner in my office with the legend 'No visits allowed during working hours', but I saw the lady actually needed help.

"Thank you." She said, smiling with difficulty.

That is when I fully assessed the extent of the damage on her face.

"Good God!" I exclaimed "Have you been in a fight or something?"

"Worse than a fight." She replied. "I have been through hell."

"What happened?" I asked, concerned.

"I was in a fight with my mate when our husband came in." she said.

"And he did not stop the fight?" I asked

"He instead removed his belt and joined her to give me a thorough beating."

"Why?" I asked perplexed. "Why would he join her, without even bothering to find out what the problem was and which of you was wrong?"

"He accused me of trying to spoil his nice juicy thing for which he had spent much money to get?"

I was shocked.

"Is that how he called his second wife?" I asked. "A thing for which he had spent much money to get?"

"Those were his very words." The aggrieved senior wife said

"And this woman did not protest?" I asked

"Protest?" Matimi said with emphasis "She rather lied to him that she had surprised me making an appointment with the man who comes taking readings from the electricity meter, and that he was giving me taxi money to meet him in some inn."

"Is that what really transpired?" I asked disturbed.

"Certainly not! I am a decent woman." she said "Instead, it is this junior mate of mine that has been messing around. I was surprised today when I saw her openly making an appointment with this worker of the National Electricity Corporation and accepting money from him, but I thought she was going too far. When I tried to advise her against it, she flared up."

"She flared up instead of listening to you?" I asked.

"She did just that and started calling me names. She said if I could satisfy my husband he would not have come for her as a second wife. But it was when she insinuated that my son was most likely a bastard child, that I could no longer hold myself back. I attacked and we started fighting."

"Now tell me," I asked "Do you really love your husband?"

"When you live with a man for all this while you are certainly bound to develop some feeling for him. I don't know whether I can call it love."

"But is there anything in him that you do not like or that you would have loved to change?" I asked cautiously.

"Many." She said. "He has nasty eating habits. He harasses and beats me often. He does not allow me to take a job and does not make available enough money for my personal needs. Finally, despite the fact that he has two wives, he still sleeps around with other women openly."

I could have added that he was almost uglier than an orangutan, but one woman's meat is another woman's poison, so I let it go.

"How did you come to marry a man with so many negative aspects as you have mentioned?" I asked "Or is it that all these negative aspects surfaced after marriage?"

"I must confess" she said "that the first time I saw him I almost ran away. I could not imagine getting married to such a man."

"Such a man?" I asked "What was wrong with him?"

"You are certainly aware of the fact that he could never pass for handsome." She said.

She was right. Faced with such a fellow, every woman's first tendency would actually be to puke

"Many men are not handsome at all." I said.

"That is true," she said "but in his case you are aware that he is virtually in a class of his own. He could be the twin brother of a gorilla."

That was close to my orangutan only slightly better.

"If you say so." I said "But you still got married to him."

"That was pressure from my parents." she said. "I come from a poor family and my parents were finding it difficult to pay my fees. He was prepared to help in the upbringing of my junior siblings. I married when I was barely nineteen years old and since then, life has been miserable."

I could imagine marriage to such a hideous dictator.

"When he was marrying the second wife, did he ask for your opinion?" I asked.

"He simply informed me that I was getting old and he had found a young girl who will become his second wife."

"Just like that?" I asked.

"Just like that." She answered.

"Now that you have come to see me" I said "what do you want me to do?"

"I want you to talk to my husband. Make him see that I am innocent."

"Let me give you some advice." I said. "It is not another woman who can come solving such a problem. You are a woman. Stand up against your husband and get the respect you deserve."

"Or get the beating of the year." She said.

"You have let yourself into that mess" I said "stand up to your husband. Get yourself a job and some degree of independence."

"That will be a very dangerous thing to do." She said.

"Then, I can't help you." I said "and I am quite busy right now. I only received you because I wanted to sympathize with your plight."

She was thoughtful for a while.

"You work," she said "and your husband allows you to?"

"Of course," I replied "I would not have allowed him to rest if I did not have a job."

"Even if I wanted to work," she said glumly "who would give me a job?"

"I could help you." I said. "You went to school, right?"

"Yes." She replied.

"Up to what level?" I asked

"I went through high school. When I was marrying, my parents insisted that I must complete high school."

"It means you have some basic qualification on which we can work despite the fact that you have been inactive for quite a number of years. Now, go home and bring me the documents. I will help you to write an application and help to follow it up."

"Thank you very much." She said. "I knew I could count on you."

That evening I told Akoni what had transpired.

"Do you want me to see Batifuomu and set him straight as to who was trying to cheat on him?"

"Not yet." I said. "Not until we have a job for Matimi. That is where you can help for now."

"I hope she will not be too choosy." Akoni said.

"I don't think so. She looked quite desperate and this seems to be the only solution."

I reflected a bit. "I only hope I am doing the right thing" I said "I would not want to look like a home wrecker."

"I hope so too." Akoni said. "Batifuomu is so full of himself, choleric and stiff. However, I know in every man, there could be some degree of flexibility. Yes, there is always some soft spot that appears when a man realizes that he has pushed a loved one to an extreme action. But does Batifuomu really feel any love for Matimi? If he does, then know that you have the right solution."

"I hope you are right." I said.

"I am a man and I understand what goes through a man's mind." Akoni said. "Some men beat their wives because they hate them. Others are stern and overbearing simply because they don't want to show the weakness in them. Thank you dear for not advising Matimi to leave. Your approach of looking for a job is better. If it works, she will have her job, and will not have to always be at home with her unpredictable mate."

"It is good to have an understanding husband like you." I said. "Do you know that you are my best friend?"

"What can I love better than being your best friend, apart from cognac?" Akoni joked.

"Cognac?" I asked "is that your second wife too?"

We both laughed over it.

The next day I met Matimi as I got to the office.

"You know, you gave me the best solution to the problem." She said. "My husband did not even notice my presence at home and stuck to his sweetheart."

"That means you have to stand up to yourself." I said. "I discussed with my husband and he is prepared to help. The only thing I will ask of you is not to mention our names to your husband when you get your job. But don't worry. If there is trouble, my husband will step in."

"Thank you very much" she said "and thank your husband for me. I will be waiting for you to call when the job is ready. Here are my documents and phone number. I would have given some money to cover expenses but depending fully on what my husband gives me, it is quite difficult."

"No problem." I said "We are prepared to help you."

After a week, Akoni landed a job for Matimi. She was going to serve as a junior clerk in one of the companies in town. I was so excited and called Matimi at once. Matimi was effusive with thanks when she got the news. Her husband had ignored her completely since the last incident with her mate and she had really gotten desperate. In support of a fellow woman, I prevailed on Akoni to lend her some money to start work with. She would need taxi money, take care of her lunch break, and assure that she had the necessary make up and other items women need to fit in well as working women. Salaries are normally paid at the end of the month so the loan was necessary.

Matimi started work and could not inform her husband because he would not talk to her. After a week she called. Her husband had found out from his second wife that she had a job. Fortunately he was informed when he was rushing for an appointment and could not react savagely on Matimi immediately. I informed Akoni.

"I will have to keep a close eye on Batifuomu." Akoni said "This is the crucial moment to convince him before he commits murder in his home."

Early the next morning, Batifuomu's first move was to give Matimi a thorough beating before going to work and to prevent her from going to work. I received a call from her boss, informing me she had not reported for work and immediately went to Batifuomu's house where I found Matimi with a black eye, a bleeding nose and swollen jaw where Batifuomu's clenched fist had landed. She looked very frightened and forlorn.

"What happened? " I asked.

"My husband gave me a terrible beating." she replied

"When?" I asked.

The blood clot around her nose was still fresh.

"This morning." she replied. "He came back home a bit late yesterday and I was already asleep and my door was locked. It appears he had gotten quite drunk before coming home and had been with some other woman. This morning I got up early to prepare and go to work. That is when he pounced on me."

"And your mate?" I asked "she did not come to help?"

"She rather laughed mockingly and made derogatory statements about stupid housewives who thought they could defy their husband and earn their own living."

"Where is your mate now?" I asked. I wanted to tell her off in no uncertain manner.

"She went out as usual, shortly after our husband left for work." Matimi replied.

"So," I said, "What do you intend to do now? You are not going to take this savagery lying down are you?"

"I really don't know what to do." she replied morosely.

"Get dressed" I said "We are going to see a doctor."

"Whatever you say." she replied.

Batifuomu had pushed her to an extreme and she was prepared to do anything.

At the doctor's she was well examined and drugs prescribed. Then we established a medical report showing the damage on her body that had resulted from the serious beatings she had received from her husband.

"Your husband thinks he is a smart lawyer," I said "but with this report, we shall have him cornered."

From the hospital we reported the matter to the police. I dropped Matimi at her job site where I explained everything to the manager. She was also a woman, and easily understood and sympathized with what our friend was going through.

Batifuomu had other plans as I was to discover. Not satisfied with having chastised his wife for taking a job, he had decided to go to her employer and insist on her being laid off from the job. Batifuomu got there an hour after I had dropped Matimi, not knowing that we had been there before him and Matimi's manager was fully aware of the fact that Matimi needed to be protected. He was thus surprised to see his battered wife at work. She had run for cover shrieking as he approached her menacingly.

By some coincidence, I had remembered that I needed to pass through a Bailiff's office and arrange for him to serve Batifuomu with the summons from the police. After I did that, I had decided to go back and see whether Matimi had overcome her trepidations and had fully calmed down and settled down to work. I had gone straight to the manager's office and found out that she was equally worried by Matimi's situation. Both of us had decided to go and see Matimi together.

As we approached Matimi's sector, we heard a shriek of distress and noticed that she had unwanted company. A huge gorilla of a man seemed to be stalking her. Just then Batifuomu turned round, probably with the intention of heading for the manager's office and expressing his objection to his wife's being employed. He was embarrassed to find a stern looking woman striding towards him. I was close behind also trying to look very stern and determined.

"I hope that is the manager's office you are coming from." Batifuomu said "I need to go and express my disgust at certain practices out here."

The manager signalled two burly guards to move over and give support and as they moved over to join us, she was now comfortable that she could cope with any violence from the hefty lawyer. She now spoke with confidence.

"What do you want here?" she asked "Don't you see that apart from trespassing, you are frightening and disturbing my workers?"

"That is my wife" Batifuomu declared "and she has no reason to be here."

"She is an employee" said the manager "and she has every reason to be here."

"And who are you?" Batifuomu asked rudely

"That is not a polite way of asking questions in a place where you are not welcome." the manager replied. "Now leave before I call the police."

"Let me warn you," Batifuomu said "I am a lawyer and you are illegally keeping my wife."

"If you are a lawyer," said the manager "then you are a very crude and dull one who knows little about the law. This woman here is an adult and free citizen of this country, and has every right to be employed and earn a living."

"You have no right to employ her without my permission." Batifuomu said stupidly.

"The law may be bad in so many things that concern the woman." I said. "We have for example, this stupid law that prohibits a married woman from traveling abroad without the permission of her husband, but in this particular case, a woman does not need permission from her husband to take a job."

"I can twist the law and nail you." Batifuomu threatened

"We shall see about that." the manager replied. "If you know anything about the law you would realize that you are trespassing. Now, take off, you rude fellow."

"You have heard her." one of the burly security guards said menacingly. "The manager says you should leave right away."

Batifuomu was weighing the situation. He probably realized that he was no match for the two security guards and his wife's manager did not look like a female that could be intimidated. I am sure he had come, thinking of meeting a fellow man but discovered a female, and women are naturally protective of their sex. I could imagine him thinking of what he would do to his wife at home.

As Batifuomu was retreating, I called after him.

"Hey wife beater!" I shouted.

He turned and looked at me with angry eyes.

"I just wish to inform you that there is a summons from the police waiting for you at the office."

I had prevailed on the police superintendent to prepare the summons for that same day at 1pm. At 1pm I was at the police office with Matimi. About five minutes later, Batifuomu strode in looking defiant and angry. He eyed us both as if given the chance, he would strangle us with his bare hands.

As he sat down Matimi's complaint was read out to him and the medical report handed over to him to see. As somebody who knew the law Batifuomu immediately realized that this was serious.

"Your wife could press charges against you," the superintendent said "but she prefers not to. All she wants is that you don't lay a finger on her again."

Batifuomu made no attempt to reply.

"This is a serious warning I am giving you." the superintendent said. She has given us the right to send the case ahead for prosecution if you dare to raise a finger against her. She is a woman, not a dog. Even dogs are not beaten like that."

Batifuomu came out of the office looking much chastised. I took Matimi to my office and coached her a bit on how to handle her husband. It was not difficult. She was already fed up with the bloke and would prefer to sue for divorce and pack out. After all, she had her job now.

Matimi turned out to be a very diligent and duty conscious worker. Years of suppression under a very dictatorial husband had made her very obedient. She was very smart too and it did not take her long to completely master her work. Akoni and I were happy that we had gotten her a job and prevailed on Batifuomu to refrain from disturbing her from working. Out of anger and frustration, Batifuomu had abandoned his matrimonial obligations towards her, and paid all his attention on the second wife, and his numerous concubines of course. For more than six months therefore, Matimi had enough time to concentrate on her job.

One day however, as we got up in the morning to go to work, Akoni received a call from Batifuomu.

"What does he want dear?" I asked after the call ended

"He says he needs to talk to me and that it is urgent."

"He did not give you any headlines?" I asked

"Don't push." Akoni said. "Let me see him and hear what his problem is. He says I should meet him at Baingeh Clinic." Akoni said.

We separated and I drove to my office.

I was concentrating on my work when the phone rang. It was Akoni.

"Hello sweet heart." he said "Could you come across immediately and meet me at Baingeh Clinic?"

"I have too much work." I complained "What is so urgent?"

"Please, do come." He pleaded "Batifuomu is in serious trouble."

"What has he been up to this time?" I asked "Has he turned on Nasah, the other wife?"

"How did you guess?" Akoni asked.

"A woman's instincts." I said. "Matimi is fully protected now and equally very cautious not to provoke anything. Batifuomu can only have problems with his second wife or one of his concubines."

"Batifuomu's second wife is here unconscious. He needs money and does not know how to tell the first wife and ask her for help, so just bring her along."

When Mawumi and Matimi finally arrived, Nasah had regained consciousness. However she still looked very shaken from the way she had been beaten up by Batifuomu. Matimi immediately rushed to her side and started examining her as if she were a loving mother examining her child.

"What actually happened?" I asked Akoni.

"That is the same question I asked Batifuomu when I arrived and have still not had a reply." Akon said.

He turned to Batifuomu

"Finally, will you tell me what actually happened?" he asked Batifuomu

"The bitch" Batifuomu said "I discovered that all along she was competing with me."

"Competing with you?" I asked "competing for what?"

"That whore has been doing everything to sleep with as many men as I do with women." he said.

"You don't mean it!" Akoni exclaimed. "And not long ago it was Matimi who was accused of sleeping with other men."

"This witch tricked me into it" Batifuomo said "Love can actually make you blind. Matimi was a very good and respectable woman all along and I should never have suspected her of cheating on me."

"So what really happened?" Akoni asked again

"I could not hold back my anger when I came back to the house suddenly and found her entangled with some dirty chap."

"You don't mean it!" Akoni exclaimed again.

"Right in my own house." Batifoumu said fuming "She probably took advantage of the fact that Matimi goes out to work and I generally work and come back late.

"Maybe she tried it just this once." Akoni said in a bid to sooth the seething anger in Batifuomu.

"Apparently, my neighbour's gate man who has rotten teeth, terribly stale breath and a wonderfully ugly face, is the only person around in the neighbourhood that has not succeeded in making love with her. This gateman told me everything."

"So when you caught her in the act you decided to punish her in no uncertain manner" Akoni asked

"But what of her lover?" I asked "Don't tell me you let him go free just because he is a man and administered all the punishment only on your wife."

"Nasah was guilty and deserved severe punishment." Batifuomu said

"The lover boy too." I insisted.

"I did not want to take on two people at once" Batifoumu said. "Nasah could have escaped and I needed to teach her a lesson."

"I suspect that you were rather scared of taking on Nasah's lover. Was he on the hefty side?" Akoni asked

"Quite." Batifoumu said "I pretended not to notice him and ignored him completely. You never know, some of these lover boys are fighters and I will not be beaten in my own house and in front of my own wife."

112

"But you caught him with your wife." I said "Remorse and guilt would have compelled him to shrink from fighting you."

"That is what you think." Batifoumu said "I am a confirmed lecher myself and we lechers feel no guilt. A lecher will rather fight back to prove to your wife that he is better than you in other ways apart from the bed."

"You virtually beat Nasah into pulp." I said

"My anger took over me and I did not care where I struck her." Batifoumu said "After several jabs, she fell unconscious. That is when I rushed her to the clinic and called for Akoni."

"What does the doctor say?" I asked

"She has gained consciousness but the doctor can only admit her and start treatment if I pay in some money, and what they have asked for is quite much. Right now I am quite broke. I know Matimi has money, but how can I approach her?"

"You are her almighty husband." I said "Simply order her to make available the money and she will obey without any hesitation."

"This is no time for joking." he said seriously "I took a loan and invested in some bad business that was brought up by Nasah's brother. I am suspecting that Nasah and her brother connived to dupe me. All my money is gone and I even mortgaged my house to get a huge loan. Now, all the money is gone and my house is at stake. I don't know how I will survive"

"Make it up with Matimi." I advised "She works and earns a good salary. Her needs have certainly not been much so she would have saved a pretty sum. Make it up with her and save the situation. I hope you now see the advantage of having a working wife."

"She won't come running if I called for her after everything I have done to her." Batifuomu said glumly.

"Mawumi could help," Akoni said "Matimi will now become the breadwinner of the home."

7

Akoni

As I got into my office one morning, I found an invitation to attend one of those meetings on gender and the emancipation of the woman. It was scheduled to take place at the town hall the following day and some popular female leaders had been listed as guest speakers. I thought of boycotting the meeting, but then decided to go.

The meeting venue was full of important looking women, all ready to contribute their quota to make the world a better place for women. The meeting started with a few papers presented on the situation of the woman and the girl child.

The first paper painted a very deplorable picture of the situation of women and girls and blamed men completely for the plight of the feminine sex. The speaker ended up by painting a dream situation of a day when there would be equal opportunity for both sexes. There was heavy applause as she stepped down from the rostrum.

The next speaker dwelled on the fact that most of the problems women faced was caused by other women. Women championed most of the old repugnant traditional atrocities like female genital mutilation. Mothers- in-law and sisters in-law would not want to see a fellow women being treated by their son or brother as an equal. Some married women lure the husbands of others knowing very well how hurtful it is for a woman to discover that her husband is cheating on her. Many spinsters, instead of looking for their own man and setting up their own home, end up as concubines to married men who normally should shower all their love only to their lawful wives.

Another speaker was rather interested in the aspect of men treating their concubines and girlfriends better than their wives at home. The time will come, she concluded when wives will be better treated and concubines will be worse off.

She also received much applause despite the fact that her approach was wrong. She was pitting married women against unmarried women while making the man a hero, whereas our common enemy here was supposed to be the man. Since I was not privileged to be a guest speaker, I kept my thoughts to myself.

After these presentations on the situation of the woman and the girl child we went into the real thing. A few points were raised on which we had to debate. I am sure I can remember some of them:

- Do you think at home you are working too much and your husband is doing little?
- Do you always cook for your husband? If you do, do you think he should also take turns in cooking? Do you do the cooking grudgingly or you are happy to do it?
- When your husband comes home drunk, do you nag, advice or help him?
- Do you think that all husbands have affairs? If you do, do you counter by dating his friends, praying that he should change or you investigate to be sure?
- Would you prefer to remain blissfully unaware of any possibility that your husband could have a girlfriend or concubine?
- Would you have preferred to be a man instead of a woman?
- Do you think you and your husband are equal?.

- Do you wash his undergarments and socks while on the other hand he touches your undergarments only when he is attempting to remove them in bed?
- Do you accept the man as the head of the family?

The meeting ended up with discussions on these topics, which produced no concrete answers. There were a few opinions though.

One participant declared that each woman should handle her own husband the way she thought best.

Another participant argued that since men were different in character and temperament, you should study your husband well and then make out how to handle him.

A third participant based her approach on the degree of love you had for your husband. Her opinion was that some women marry a man because they love him deeply while others accept the man simply because he was the only one who came proposing. You handle the man according to your degree of love for him.

There was yet another school of thought who held that there should be an even gender balance. You take turns in cooking, and doing all the house hold chores that men generally abandon to the women. One of the women even insisted that it was wrong to give up your maiden name in marriage to go bearing some other blokes name simply because he is your husband. The debate was quite hot. The issue of accepting the man as the head of the family was equally hotly debated.

Most of us went home more confused. We had gained virtually nothing concrete from the workshop. That evening I recounted everything to Akoni and he listened carefully to the end.

"What do you think?" I asked.

117

"Women have a certain position in society which we should accept". He said. "A woman cannot become a man and a man cannot become a woman. Your sex determines certain traits, likes and dislikes behavioural tendencies etc. You see, most arguments that women bring up about the plight of the woman are baseless."

"Is that your opinion or you read it somewhere?" I joked.

He smiled back.

"If you look deeply into the problems of one woman, you will discover that they have been caused by another woman. Many women don't want to see their colleagues happy. Some easily seize a lover from another woman or flirt with a friend's husband. Why would a woman insist on going out with a friend's husband? Things have gotten to an extent that it is difficult to trust a woman."

"Have you finished?" I asked.

"What else is there to say?" He answered. "Women are the cause of their problems."

"You have simply spoken like a man." I said. "Would you blame a caring woman for being battered by a brute husband? Would you blame a young beautiful wife for being forced into the bed of another man just because he is her boss? Would you blame a woman for suing for divorce or abandoning the home because a lecher of a husband is transforming the home into a brothel? There are so many questions whose answers point at the man as the main cause of women's woes"

"There could be a few exceptions" Akoni said stubbornly, but look well and you will find a woman behind each cause. Some men leave their wives and go for harlots because they are there and harlots are women. A man may switch to another woman because his own wife pushes him away, through nagging or refusal to offer sex etc. Then, look at this employment situation. Women entice the boss for employment, promotion and good treatment at work."

"That is a very limited way of thinking." I said. "I am talking of various ills imposed upon the woman by male influence, and negative aspects in cultures and tradition that are determined by men. Is it not the man who imposed such horrible things as female genital mutilation, wearing of the veil, kowtowing before the man, bride price and dowry, forced marriages, rape and sexual violence etc?.

"There you have a point." Akoni admitted. "Certain societal norms or tendencies imposed by men have forced women into prostitution and other deplorable ways of life. You are right dear; men are behind most of the woes of women."

"Thanks dear." I said.

"But I forgot to add that men do these things with the complicity of some women." He added.

"You have come back to your first stand." I pointed out.

"Let's look at a simple thing like female genital mutilation." Akoni said. "It was instituted by men because they wanted to guarantee the fidelity of their wives. You see, the men enjoyed sex but did not consider the fact that a woman too had the right to enjoy sex. The man brought up the idea of slicing off the clitoris of every little girl with the belief that when she grows up to become a wife, she would not enjoy sex without it. That way, she will not be interested in sleeping around with other men. She will only accept sex with her husband as a duty. In some tribes in Sudan, they stitched the lips of the vagina of a small girl to prevent her from having sex before marriage. These brutal acts were however championed by women, who themselves carried out

119

these hideous operations and made sure that every female was forced to pass through it."

"You accept that such heinous ideas are developed by men before they drag women into it?" I asked.

"I just needed to argue with you a bit." Akoni said "For a long time we have been agreeing on everything.